THE HUNGER
AND ECSTASY OF
VAMPIRES

THE HUNGER AND ECSTASY OF VAMPIRES

A NOVEL BY

BRIAN STABLEFORD

MARK V. ZIESING BOOKS
SHINGLETOWN, CA • 1996

THE HUNGER AND ECSTASY OF VAMPIRES
© *1996 by Brian Stableford*

Published by
Mark V. Ziesing
Post Office Box 76
Shingletown, CA 96088

Manufactured in the
United States of American

FIRST EDITION

Cover painting and hand lettering by Arnie Fenner

SIGNED LIMITED EDITION:
ISBN 0-929480-81-3
TRADE EDITION:
ISBN 0-929480-80-5
LIBRARY OF CONGRESS:
95-062272

THE HUNGER AND ECSTASY OF VAMPIRES

Prologue

The air above the city was uncommonly clear and the stars shone brightly. The moon was full, and visibility was good even though the nearest gas-light was a hundred metres away.

Jean Lorrain disapproved of *Monsieur le Comte's* insistence—in frank defiance of convention—that the duel must be fought *before* dawn, but he grudgingly admitted to himself that there was light enough. In fact, as he and Octave Uzanne walked across the dewy grass to meet Mourier's seconds he felt alarmingly conspicuous, as if he had unwittingly exposed himself to some attentive eye whose attention he had done better to avoid. There was something about this business that filled him with a dire and horrible unease. It seemed oddly like a premonition of some future disaster. He had never experienced such a sensation before, even when he had been the one appointed to fire the gun.

This was the very spot where Lorrain had faced Guy de Maupassant not so long after first arriving in Paris, and even

THE HUNGER AND ECSTASY OF VAMPIRES

though he had known Guy since childhood he had not been absolutely sure that the elder writer would discharge his pistol harmlessly into the ground, as modern etiquette demanded. He had been anxious then—near sick with anxiety, in fact—but he had not felt the way he did now, weak at the knees with superstitious dread. Perhaps it was merely a delayed effect of the ether, which had filled his house with ghosts as soon as he had started taking it; not all of them had had been laid to rest when he had stopped.

One of Mourier's men opened the box to display the ancient pistols resting within. Lorrain, who was no expert judge of weapons, did not bother to inspect them closely; he was happy to presume that they were identical. Uzanne likewise waved them away with barely a glance.

Mourier's senior second—a white-haired man whose bearing was sternly military—took Lorrain to one side, with an exaggerated pantomime of discretion, to say: "I wonder if all this is really necessary. *Monsieur* Mourier has authorized me to say that he had no intention of causing mortal offence. He wishes it to be known that he repeated the rumour only to comment on its utter absurdity, not with the intention of spreading it further. If *Monsieur le Comte* wishes to deal with the author of the rumour he must look elsewhere."

Mourier is frightened, Lorrain thought. *Because Monsieur le Comte is not a Frenchman, let alone a Parisian, Mourier cannot be sure that he will follow the unwritten law.* Aloud, he said: "I fear that *Monsieur le Comte* has instructed me not to accept an apology."

The old soldier curled his lip in obvious distaste. At first, Lorrain thought that it was he who had prompted the distaste—he was certain that the man had recognised him, although he had not the slightest idea who he was—but he realised when the soldier continued that it was Mourier's instructions that were sticking in his throat.

"*Monsieur* Mourier has asked me to make it perfectly clear that he does not believe there are such things as vampires, and that he used the word in connection with *Monsieur le Comte* simply to make clear the absurdity of any such belief. He has also asked me to say that he had no intention of implying that *Monsieur le Comte* is using an assumed name."

Mourier is very frightened indeed, Lorrain thought. *Even his seconds feel that he should not go to such lengths of self-abasement. In any case, he is wrong. France is full of vampires; I have seen them myself, and have joined their company, gathering at the abattoir gate in the rue de Flandre before dawn's first light. As long as consumption runs riot through the land and as long as there are doctors who believe that fresh ox-blood is an effective treatment there will be no shortage of vampires here. The doctors are quacks, of course—blood has no more virtue than ether, although it does not visit a man with quite so many phantoms—but wherever there is ill-heath there will always be quacks. As for assumed names, that is a trivial matter. I wear one myself, at my father's command—although, in the end, it was he and not I who dragged the name Duval in the dirt.*

"Well?" snapped the military man, impatient for his reply.

Lorrain coughed into his hand, and felt flecks of bloody sputum hit his palm. He felt almost relieved, although he had not coughed blood for some weeks. It reassured him that the terrible dread which had possession of him must be physical after all. "I fear," he murmured, hoarsely, "that *Monsieur le Comte* will not depart without exchanging shots. It is all most unfortunate, I confess, but *Monsieur le Comte* has been pursued by evil rumours through half the capitals in Europe, and these whispers have caused him considerable pain. He is perfectly able to ignore jests of an ordinary kind which link his name with certain young women, but there is one particular name which causes him particular hurt, and that is Laura Vambery's. He had not thought to hear it mentioned here in Paris, given that the incident happened long ago and in another country, and it wounded him deeply. He would surely admit, as a matter of mere probability, that Monsieur Mourier did not intend to charge him with direct responsibility for the girl's death, let alone of drinking her life's blood, but he feels that unless he responds in a firm and definite way to your friend's carelessness others might feel comfortable in making similarly vile insinuations."

Mourier's second sighed, in a very contrived and ostentatious fashion—but there was real anxiety in his eyes. "*Monsieur le Comte* does understand, I suppose, that this is 1894, not 1794, and that whatever the situation in his homeland might be, the courts of France have become very serious in their opposition to *private settlements*."

This, Lorrain knew, was the true heart of the matter. "*Monsieur le Comte* may not be a Parisian," he said, with malicious frostiness, "but he is well enough acquainted with the direction in which the march of progress is taking our society. He knows full well that we are here as a matter of honour, not to attempt murder. I can assure you that if his opponent were, let us say, accidentally to discharge his weapon without fully raising it, so that the ball went harmlessly to earth, *Monsieur le Comte* would not dream of attempting to fire a fatal shot in return."

The old soldier actually laughed, albeit softly. His relief was palpable. He even raised his open-palmed hand in an amicable gesture. "I confess that I am glad to hear it," he said, his voice hardly above a whisper. "In the days of my youth, duels were fought authentically, and the law knew far better than to interfere—but nothing has been the same since that damned humiliating war. Even the Prussians would be ashamed had they known how deeply France would be scarred by it. What kind of a future are we making for ourselves, when men who meet on the field of honour no longer dare to aim their guns? Sometimes I fear that in refusing to dig secret graves for our boldest and best, we may be digging a grave for all mankind." He turned way as soon as he had finished speaking, as if he regretted his own loquacity.

He is rambling! Lorrain thought. *He is as horridly disturbed as I am—as we all are! All, that is, except Monsieur le Comte.*

By now the pistols had been conveyed to the combatants by Octave Uzanne and Mourier's junior second, and the selection made. It was the military man who placed the adversaries carefully back to back, and made certain that they knew exactly when to walk, and exactly at what point to turn. There was nothing for Lorrain to do now but stand back and watch.

Again that feeling of *premonition* swept over him, and he could not help shuddering. He hoped that the curious and malevolent imp which stirred in his belly was a mere ache, but feared that it might be a kind of thirst—whether for ether, or for warm blood, he dared not hazard a guess.

Lorrain watched the two gentlemen take their measured paces. *Monsieur le Comte* was not the taller of the two, nor the younger, but he seemed nevertheless to be the more commanding figure. The rumours which pursued him alleged that he was an accomplished mesmerist as well as a fiend, and in spite of the fact that there was nothing in the least intimidating about his ordinary gaze, Lorrain found that easy enough to believe. The man from the East seemed to be in a kind of trance now, as if his mind had slipped into some uncommon mode of consciousness which permitted a concentration as absolute as that which resulted from obsessive monomania. The precision with which he turned to face his opponent at the apposite moment was smoothly mechanical.

Mourier began to raise his arm, trying to hold it as straight as a ramrod but failing miserably. His terror was embarrassingly frank. Long before it reached the horizontal the progress of the trembling arm was interrupted, and Mourier allowed it to fall back. The arm was limp when the pistol in his hand went off, and the ball discharged harmlessly into the turf no more than half a metre from his toes.

After that, there was nothing for Mourier to do but wait. He tried to look his opponent in the eye, but he could not do it.

No flicker of a smile passed across the face of *Monsieur le Comte* on account of the fact that he could not now be hurt. His own pistol was already raised, and it pointed unwaveringly at his opponent's heart—but then, with scrupulous politeness, *Monsieur le Comte* let the barrel droop, so that the weapon was angled conspicuously downwards, pointing at the spot from which the two men had stood back-to-back.

He fired.

Mourier fell, clutching his throat.

THE HUNGER AND ECSTASY OF VAMPIRES

Lorrain could not restrain a cry of astonishment and anguish—a cry echoed by Uzanne and the younger of Mourier's seconds. Even the old soldier started with amazement and exclaimed in horror. For a moment or two, Lorrain took leave to wonder whether some cruel supernatural agency had redirected *Monsieur le Comte's* bullet. Even when he had realised, belatedly, that the missile must have struck a stone, he could not help but wonder whether *Monsieur le Comte* might actually have *aimed* at the stone, calculating that the ricochet would strike his opponent in the heart. Such a trick was surely impossible—and yet, *Monsieur le Comte* still seemed quite impassive. Neither surprise nor alarm was evident in his stony expression. He stood stock still, waiting.

Mourier's seconds were already hard at work when Lorrain and Uzanne reached them. The old soldier was desperately attempting to stem the flow of blood from the wound which had opened Mourier's windpipe, although his lace-edged handkerchief was woefully inadequate to the task. Lorrain had seen many a bloodstained handkerchief in his time, but never one so red and sodden as this one.

The white-haired man looked up. "Go, you fool!" he said, in a tortured voice. "Get your man away from here, and out of Paris. Send him home by the fastest available route. It matters not that at all that the killing was an accident, a chance in a million. There will be hell to pay, and if your friend does not want rumours of vampirism and the name of Laura Vambery bandied about in open court, he had better not set foot in France for a very long time."

Lorrain ran back to *Monsieur le Comte*, resentfully aware of the fact that he and Uzanne hardly knew the man, and had only consented to be his seconds because they had been asked so urgently. *Monsieur le Comte* still had the weapon in his hand, and did not drop it when Lorrain urged him to flee for his life—but he condescended to return to his coach and give the necessary instructions to his German coachman.

Lorrain and Uzanne got into the carriage behind him, and took their places to either side of him as the horses took it away, hurrying beneath the whip. No one spoke. *Monsieur le Comte* offered no explanation or apology—he seemed to be lost in a private world of his own, hardly belonging to this one at all. Before the rumours had arrived in his wake he had seemed the most charming of men—one of those who sparkled beneath the brilliant light of chandeliers, perfectly at home in the *salons* which be graced with his presence—but he was very different now.

The carriage set the two friends down in the rue de Courty while dawn was just beginning to tint the sky. Lorrain had not seen that first light since the days when he had played the vampire in the rue de Flandre and it reminded him forcibly of the odour and taste of blood, and of the effort that had been required to force the warm liquid down while his gorge rose in rebellion against its foulness.

"I would not like to be a vampire," he said to Uzanne. "To wear the mask of a common man, while nurturing some dark and precious secret identity, would be one thing—but to live on blood and blood alone would be another. I would rather let the fever consume me."

Uzanne looked at him very strangely—as well he might, considering that he had not been party to Lorrain's train of thought. "You had best be careful in using that word," he said. "We have just seen a man die because he repeated it."

THE HUNGER AND ECSTASY OF VAMPIRES

"Have I ever been careful?" Lorrain asked him, only realising when he smiled that the feeling of dread had left him. As light possessed the sky, the pall that had hung over him was lifting, letting him free.

"No," his friend admitted, "you never have. Perhaps you should—or one day, it might be you that dawn finds lying there, nourishing the soil with your rich Norman blood. What a tragedy that would be, when you have not yet written your masterpiece! If you find room in it for *Monsieur le Comte*, as you have found room for so many others, you must be certain to disguise him well."

"I doubt if any writer who had met him could resist the temptation," Lorrain answered. "But you are right—he would have to be heavily disguised—and not by any mere reversal of his name."

They went into the house together, and drank brandy until mama awoke and asked her wayward son exactly where he had been all night.

"Helping a friend in need," he said, although he knew that she would not believe him.

* * * *

1

"Do you know Professor Edward Copplestone?" Oscar Wilde asked me, as he sipped appreciatively from his glass. It contained absinthe which I had smuggled in from Paris for him. We were dining at Roche's in Soho, but our host made no objection to the absinthe. *An Ideal Husband* had just started its run, to universal acclaim, and Wilde could do no wrong within those or any other walls.

I had been less than a month in London, and knew hardly anyone, so I denied it almost without thinking.

"He dines here sometimes," said Wilde, "but he cannot really be considered a member of our set. He is a great traveller, and tells extravagant tales of his adventures in parts of the world of which most of us have never heard. Some of his stories may even be true, although that hardly matters. He is the only man I know who can speak with casual familiarity about the hinterlands of Siberia and the Mongol lands."

That struck a chord. There was another man I knew who was widely travelled in the Far East, and liked to tell dubious traveller's tales. "Perhaps I *have* heard the name," I conceded, controlling the impulse to scowl which always assailed me when anything recalled the name of Arminius Vambery to my mind.

THE HUNGER AND ECSTASY OF VAMPIRES

"You will find it extensively acknowledged in the notes and bibliographies of Tylor's *Primitive Culture* and Frazer's *Golden Bough*," said Wilde, airily—although I suspected that he had read neither book. "He is a self-supposed expert on primitive religion and magic, with particular reference to shamanistic cults, but he is by no means a Dryasdust. Quite a dreamer, in his way. No stranger to the opium dens of Limehouse, and rumour can usually be trusted—except, of course, when it turns its attention to me."

This news was mildly reassuring. It was entirely probable that such a man might know Arminius Vambery by repute, but Vambery was unlikely to have gone out of his way to pour out his troubled heart to a man reputed to be a dope fiend. Like most sober madmen of impeccable reputation, Vambery had little tolerance of delusions born of conscious artifice of those accused of courting them. Vambery was the kind of man who trusted rumours—especially those he had invented himself.

"Why do you ask whether I know this Copplestone?" I asked.

"Because he has written me a curious letter saying that he has a very strange report to make and would be grateful for my presence. He goes on to say that he considers me one of the most intelligent and open-minded men in London—I cannot imagine who else he has in mind—and that he would prize my opinion of what he has to say most highly. He requests me to bring an acquaintance as wise and as wide-eyed as myself. It is a description which could hardly apply to Bosie, or even to Robbie, and I naturally thought of you. Will you come with me, if you are not busy? The invitation is for tomorrow evening."

THE HUNGER AND ECSTASY OF VAMPIRES

"You hardly know me," I murmured. "How do you know that I fit the requirements?" I was fully in agreement with the estimate of my intellectual acumen, but I suspected that Wilde had only 'naturally thought of me' because I happened to be dining with him that evening.

"I was impressed the first time we met, in Paris," he said. "You seemed to have a view of the world of men so clear and so cynical that I could hardly believe you were part of it. It is true that we have never talked at great length about deep matters, but I am always impulsive in my judgments and I am very rarely wrong. Will you come?"

I agreed to go with him. How could I possibly have refused? In any case, I was becoming hungry for new amusement. London seemed unbelievably dull after Paris, which I had left with such a sudden wrench. It is never a good idea for an individual of my kind to stay in one place for long, but I never regretted leaving a city more than I regretted leaving Paris. On the other hand, London was not entirely devoid of advantages. One could buy a slumgirl for a shilling, and a passably pretty one at that; we who are obliged by restless nature and the harassment of vile slanders to be forever on the move must be grateful for every opportunity which a city has to offer.

"Who else will be there?" I asked.

"I really have no idea. The only other name Copplestone mentions in his letter to me is Bram Stoker's—and that is only to say that Stoker is in Ireland just now, and cannot possibly come. Copplestone does not explain why he thinks Stoker might have been a suitable candidate for inclusion; personally, I have always considered his mind to be conspicuously second-rate."

THE HUNGER AND ECSTASY OF VAMPIRES

I had laid down my fork rather abruptly at the first mention of Stoker's name. I had, in any case, only been toying with my food. I sipped a little water from my glass, but the attempt to cover up my reaction failed. Wilde must have seen my reaction immediately, and was wise enough to be surprised. He did not know me well, but he had observed that I rarely react intemperately to anything.

"Do you know Stoker at all?" he asked, curiously. "He is Henry Irving's factotum—his strong right arm, I suppose he would say."

"I have never met him," I said, in a neutral tone.

"I have seen little of him lately myself," said Wilde, "although I was a regular visitor to his home when he first moved to London. He was at Trinity before me, you know, and he was still working in Dublin when I went up. My father befriended him, and even my mother condescended to like him a little. He married a girl of whom I was exceedingly fond and I was never able to forgive his temerity. The fact that we are now in rival camps, theatrically speaking, only serves to add new insult to the old injury."

I was not in the least interested in the petty politics of the English theatre. I had heard far too much gossip about theatrical matters while staying with Lorrain, and I had had my fill of paeans of praise offered up to the divinity of Sarah Bernhardt. I knew, though, that Stoker was one of the people Arminius Vambery had talked to when he was in London; Stoker had invited him to address a meeting of the Beefsteak Club, where he had waxed lyrical on the subject of vampirism. If Stoker and Copplestone were acquainted, it was possible that Copplestone might have been present. After what had happened in Paris, I wanted to steer well clear of anyone who

THE HUNGER AND ECSTASY OF VAMPIRES

might conceivably have occasion—with whatever motive—to mention the name of Laura Vambery. But I had already accepted Wilde's invitation, and it seemed that Stoker would not actually be present. I thought it best to change the subject.

"Shall we share a carriage?" I asked. "I shall be happy to collect you, if you wish. Where does Copplestone live?"

"On the south side of the park—Regent's Park, that is, not Hyde Park. Yes, I'd be grateful if you could collect me from the Haymarket; it will be easier to tear myself away from my friends, my duties and my admirers if I know that I am impatiently awaited by a stern aristocrat. We are expected at eight. I do hope that it will be amusing. Travellers' tales have become far less interesting since Stanley let so much dismal light into the delicately dark heart of Africa, and the steady march of geographical science is slowly strangling the spirit of wild romance, but if there is any forgotten corner of the globe still rich with gorgeous mystery, Ned Copplestone is more than likely to have found it. If he intends to test our credulity, we may be reasonably sure that it will be well and truly tested, perhaps to delicious destruction."

Even though I knew full well that there were more things in Heaven and earth than were dreamt of in Oscar Wilde's philosophy, I did not think of myself as a gullible individual, and I was inclined to think that listening to a story which tested my credulity to destruction would be a waste of time—but I put my reservations firmly aside, and resolved to do my very best to play the part which had been allocated to me: that of a man of the world, clear-sighted and open-minded.

I little suspected what unprecedented demands that role would make of me in the nights which followed.

2

I called for Wilde at the appropriate hour but he was—as always—late. I had to sit in my carriage for a quarter of an hour, watching the crowds go by.

The famous London fog had condescended to leave the city unblanketed for once, and the frost had not yet begun to glitter upon the pavements. The chestnut-roasting season was well past by now and most of the brazier-men were hawking baked potatoes, whose odour was not quite so astringent. The crowd was as good a quality as one could expect to find in London out of season, but they seemed a tawdry gaggle by comparison with the excited throngs of Paris's Latin Quarter. My mood was such that they seemed more than usually like cattle trooping to the barn, or laying-hens milling about their carelessly-scattered corn. I was glad when Wilde finally consented to appear.

As we bowled along Regent Street, Wilde lost himself in some interminable anecdote, and for once his brilliance seemed slightly off-key, but he was in such good heart that he slowly roused me from my torpor of indolence. By the time we reached the fringes of the park I felt quite ready to face the challenge of the long winter night.

THE HUNGER AND ECSTASY OF VAMPIRES

Inevitably, we were the last to arrive, although my coachman had contrived to make up some of the time we had lost by showing his usual scant regard for the convenience of other road-users.

Wilde's enthusiasm seemed to falter slightly when he saw the remainder of the company gathered in Copplestone's waiting-room. He doubtless wondered what judgments had been made of *their* intelligence by way of polite enticement. He introduced me to Copplestone, who—mercifully—showed no flicker of recognition at the mention of my name.

Copplestone was a tall, gaunt man who had doubtless been more solidly-built in his younger days, but who seemed to find the advancing years uncommonly burdensome. He was not unduly wrinkled, but his complexion seemed curiously jaundiced and his handshake was far from firm. Politeness forbade me from saying so but he really did not look well, and I wondered whether he ought to have postponed his story-telling until he had recovered more of his colour and strength.

I had to concur with Wilde's unvoiced judgment that our fellow-guests did not appear at first glance to be a coterie of the most intelligent and open-minded men in England. They seemed, in fact, to comprise an assembly of eccentrics. I dare say, however, that there was more than one among them who felt that Wilde and I increased the bizarrerie of the gathering rather than adding a necessary counterweight of wise sobriety. Wilde proved, once he had removed his coat, to be dressed as flamboyantly as usual, although the green carnation in his lapel was made of silk and crepe paper. I, of course, was a foreigner—and a Count, at that—and needed no artificial aids to appear exotic in English eyes.

THE HUNGER AND ECSTASY OF VAMPIRES

While Copplestone introduced me to the others I searched anxiously for any sign or symptom which might testify to the arrival in London of scurrilous gossip, but there was nothing. If any of them had heard of the Mourier affair they were models of discretion.

The first man to whom I was presented was a stout and stolid doctor who had served in India. He seemed a man of common sense rather than exceptional cleverness, but he was the only man present who seemed to have been long acquainted with Copplestone. Copplestone referred to him as an an 'invaluable supporter' but also as an 'unwilling collaborator', and I gathered that the doctor had his own reservations about our host's physical condition.

Like Wilde, the doctor had been invited to bring a companion, and the man who accompanied him was tall and distinguished, though not particularly well-dressed. He seemed grave almost to the point of melancholy, and I was struck by the strange acuity of his grey eyes. Nothing was said concerning his station in life but he greeted me politely.

I was then introduced to two young men, perhaps not out of their twenties. The first of them was a study in contradictions. He was not thin, but the peculiar softness of his flesh gave the impression that he had recently been very lean indeed, and was filling out for the first time. His complexion was naturally pale, but he pinked very easily, and a hectic flush seemed to be continually ebbing and flowing from his cheeks. There was a slight feverish glint in his eye which suggested that he was not entirely well, although he was by no means as debilitated as our host. It was evident that Copplestone had never clapped eyes on him before, and that it was his companion to whom the professor had actually written.

THE HUNGER AND ECSTASY OF VAMPIRES

The second young man could hardly have looked more different. He was dark and curly-haired, with perhaps a touch of creole about him. Copplestone explained that he had but recently returned to London after spending some time as a schoolmaster in Derbyshire, but that Wilde knew him slightly and would doubtless be glad to see him again. Wilde obediently pantomimed the pleasure of an old acquaintance joyously renewed, but it did not seem to me that their friendship could ever have been intimate. Wilde knew so many young men that he must have found it hard to remember their names.

I judged from snippets of conversation which I barely had time to overhear that the two young men were not very well acquainted with one anther, but that they had many interests in common. Both seemed to have studied medicine, or at least biological science, and both had apparently served as teachers before finally choosing to devote themselves to the precarious life of the pen.

There was only one man in the room who presented incontrovertible evidence to the naked eye that he was older than Copplestone; he seemed to be in his mid-sixties, and his flowing beard was white, but he was still healthy. He was clearly a man of means, and also a man of science. I would presumably have recognised his name immediately had I been well versed in science, but science has always seemed to me to be very much a day-time product, and those who invariably keep late hours—as I do—tend to be thrust more often into the company of men of Wilde's or Jean Lorrain's stripe. This was the only man in the room with a title of any sort, but Copplestone did not say whether it was a baronetcy or a knighthood earned by public service; he did, however, mention that the old gentleman was as well-known for his exploits in association with the Society for Psychical Research as for more material work. This did not make me any more enthusiastic to cultivate his acquaintance.

The final member of the party, who had been brought as a companion by the white-haired man of science, was a dark-haired man of science. Copplestone seemed to think that we might get along famously together, presumably because we both had European accents, but it was obvious to the two of us, if to no one else, that we came from nations which had so little in common as never even to have fought a war. In any case, this moustachioed worthy candidly explained that he was an American by adoption, and had renounced his European identity in order to give his allegiance entirely to the American spirit of free enterprise. I was not sure exactly what this implied, but I gathered that it had something to do with the profits one could make out of the sale of patents.

I concluded, on due consideration, that although we comprised an exceedingly peculiar crew, we nevertheless constituted a team as well-qualified as any to pass judgment on an exotic and challenging report.

When I had the opportunity to stand aside for a few moments with Wilde he was quick to give me the benefit of his own judgment. "We can expect little in the way of ready wit from the men of science," he told me. "They will play their part very earnestly—but some such counterweight of sanity may be necessary, given that our remaining companions have no shortage of romance in heir souls."

"Have you read the work of either of the young men?" I asked.

"Not a word. I have heard rumour of them both, and the more personable of the two urged me to look at some of his tales, but I never found the time. The one who blushes so hectically is said to have produced some very pretty fancies about the future evolution of the race and the probability of its extinction. He has studied under Huxley, I believe, but he has absorbed the ideas without the rugged optimism. The third literary man is far more famous than either. *Everyone* has read his work."

It was news to me that there was a third literary man present. "Are you talking about the grey-eyed man?" I asked.

"No—that is, not directly. I meant the doctor, who has published several novels and a long series of short stories in a periodical called *The Strand*. The stories chronicle the adventures of a consulting detective: a master of ratiocination, who solves puzzles by observing clues that less sensitive men invariably miss. The appearance, quirks and mannerisms of the detective in question are said to be closely based on those of his grey-eyed friend—like your friend Lorrain, who annoyed Maupassant by putting him into one of his novels, the doctor prefers to paint his pen-portraits from life. Unfortunately, his friend is said to have become so entranced with the doctor's literary confections as to have convinced himself that he really is a great detective. He is only recently returned from a rest-cure in Switzerland. Rumour has it that it was forced upon him by a breakdown which he suffered when the doctor—perhaps hoping to dispel his delusion—killed off the character a little over a year ago. Perhaps he is cured—but perhaps he has convinced himself that the great detective is not dead after all and is merely in hiding, awaiting his chance to emerge from obscurity by solving a mystery deeper and more deadly than any he has ever faced before. Did you remark the strange glint in his eye?"

"I did. He certainly has a disconcerting stare—if he has the intelligence to go with it he must be a man to be reckoned with."

"It is more likely to be the effect of a new drug—a derivative of opium. He is supposed too have broken the habit while he was away, but....some habits are hard to break. Has poor Lorrain given up drinking ether, by the way?"

"I believe he has," I reported. "I think he has had enough of physicians, for now, and is more disposed to place himself in the hands of a good surgeon. But as you say, some habits are hard to break."

"I am interested to see that Copplestone has invited no clergyman, nor anyone of the legalistic turn of mind," Wilde said. "To my mind, that is evidence that he has an altogether sensible notion of trust and trustworthiness."

That was a judgment with which I concurred, but I did not have a chance to say so; we were already being ushered into the dining-room. Copplestone had the grace to feed his guests well, and to lay out a burgundy of very tolerable vintage before setting forth to tax their credulity but I—as was my habit—ate very little and drank even less, although I made a polite show of participation in the pleasures of the meal. I had been seated between the younger man of science and the doctor, opposite the grey-eyed man, so I was not ideally placed for conversation. Fortunately, Wilde son took charge of the occasion and held the entire company in thrall with anecdotes regarding the production of *An Ideal Husband*, the writing of *The Importance of Being Earnest* and the appalling behaviour of the Marquess of Queensberry.

It was not until the port was being passed that the professor introduced the serious business of the evening—by which time he seemed a little stronger than he had before the meal. I settled back in my oaken chair, ready and eager to be entertained—although I suspected that Wilde's might be a difficult act for him to follow.

I need not have worried. Despite the enormous difference in their styles, Edward Copplestone proved easily capable of putting on a fascinating show.

3

"Some of you," said Copplestone, "will already know something about the studies which have been my life's work. Some of you may even have read one or other of my monographs on the religious rites and magical practices of various exotic tribes. We are inclined to call such tribes primitive, partly on account of the fact that they indulge in un-Christian rites and un-scientific practices, but it has long been my opinion that our condescension is not entirely justified. In my admittedly-blasphemous view, Christianity has no more claim to truthfulness than any pagan faith, while modern science, in so savagely condemning the occult studies which not so long ago gave birth to it, has thrown out more than one baby with the bathwater.

"My published writings on tribal magic and divination have always been scrupulously sceptical—my reputation as a natural philosopher would have been reduced to tatters had they shown the least trace of credulity—but my private thoughts have ever been prepared to entertain hypotheses as to the shy truths which might lie hidden in the undergrowth of superstition. I have been particularly interested in the various means used by tribal magicians to obtain knowledge of the future.

THE HUNGER AND ECSTASY OF VAMPIRES

"The history of prophecy is littered with ignominious failures—and the prophecies in which, as Christian men, we are supposed to invest our faith are as ignominious as any—but I have seen enough in my travels to convince me that there are indeed some men who have the innate gift of foresight, and that there are chemical methods by which such natural gifts may be enhanced. I have long thought it probable that the application of proper scientific method to the study of such men and such chemical compounds would rapidly produce a way of inducing more accurate and more far-reaching visions of futurity.

"In saying this, I remain well aware of certain philosophical problems which arise in connection with the notion of precognition, and of certain psychological problems which inevitably confuse the visionary process. I have no wish to insult the intelligence of men like yourselves by lecturing you, but I would like to comment very briefly on both these kinds of problems in order to prepare the ground for the story which I have to tell.

"Throughout my adult life I have held firm to the belief that if the principles of causality which we have recognised since Newton's time are true, then the future must be, at least in principle, foreseeable and predictable. I have always taken it for granted that if the future flows from the present by virtue of inviolable physical laws, it must do so according to a destiny *mapped out*, as it were, since time immemorial. I took it for granted, too, that if the future really is mappable, then there must be a sense in which it already exists; if its shape is already fixed, then that shape must in some sense be *perceptible*, not in the uncertain fog of the speculative imagination, but in actuality. In the book of destiny, the moments which make up the history of the universe must lie next to one another like slender leaves, each one ready for inspection if only a man—or any other creature—were somehow able to step outside the ordinary course of his own procession."

The white-bearded man leaned forward at this point and opened his mouth to interrupt—to protest, I suppose, that there was a contradiction here, in that one could not simultaneously hold a belief in destiny and yet speak of creatures stepping outside it—but Copplestone held up a hand to forestall him.

"I am aware of the paradoxes implicit in the idea," said the professor, "and of the vicious circularity inherent in the supposition that a man may step outside the course of his destiny if, and only if, he is destined to do it. I was never satisfied with that, and have ever been impatient with the twists and turns of the labyrinth of pure conjecture. I always desired to make an *experiment* which might guide me to the heart of the philosophical maze. Rather than be content with demonstrating the impossibility of looking into the future *a priori*, I wanted to make the best effort I could actually to do it, so that I might have the leisure afterwards to examine the implications of what I had been able to do.

"It seemed to me, on the basis of my studies of drug-enhanced precognition in tribal societies, that these magicians sometimes *did* obtain true knowledge of the future, but were almost never able to profit from it. One reason for this, I perceived, was that the true knowledge which they obtained was invariably alloyed with extraneous material which frequently led to its misinterpretation. After long study I concluded that the organ of foresight—the 'sixth sense', if you will admit the term—is that which engages in the ordinary business of *dreaming*, and that its sensory function is confused by other *expressive* functions linked to the passions. In brief, our usually-meagre powers of precognition are so polluted, perverted and confused by our hopes, fears and fancies that it is normally impossible to separate truth from fantasy until the event which was dimly foreseen actually comes to pass, thus revealing the previously-hidden meaning of the precognitive vision."

I have heard all this before, I reflected. *It has been the substance of countless intoxicated debates in inns and coffee-houses. Can there really be anything new to add to it?* I glanced at the paler of the young men, and saw that he too had the look of one who had heard it all before, and found its repetition here and now a little annoying. I permitted myself a little smile; he had not yet learned the virtues of patience and relaxation. Were he lucky enough to live as long as I had, he would doubtless become less hectic of temperament.

Copplestone had not paused; he was fully in the grip of what seemed to me suspiciously like alcoholic eloquence. "It was evident to me from my extensive studies of shamanistic and related practices," he went on, "that the enhancement of visionary precognition by appropriate drugs could not entirely filter out this psychological pollution, no matter how powerfully the compounds increased the power of the sensory function—but I hoped that it might at least be minimized if the optimum combination of drugs could be found.

"Each of the tribes which I studied had to rely on the bounty of nature to supply enhancing drugs. The Siberians use agaric mushrooms, the Mexicans use *peyotl*, the Mongolians use opium derivatives. I, by contrast, had the double advantage of being able to collect and combine all these different kinds of compounds, and of being able to refine and modify them using the recently-evolved techniques of organic chemistry.

"This was what I set out to do: to discover the mechanics of a modern Delphic oracle, more powerful than any known to history. I set out to find the most reliable possible means of dividing the curtain which normally confined me within the sequence of my living moments, so that I might peer through the breach into the world which is to come. By this means I hoped to discover, among other things, whether what I had long taken for granted was actually true: whether the future glimpsed by authentic seers is, in fact, an immutable future of *destiny* which they are quite unable to affect in any way despite their foresight of it; or whether it is merely a future of *contingency*, which might yet be altered or averted if they were able to act upon their precognition."

This time he did pause, and he rang a bell to summon his manservant. This hero had single-handedly carried the food which we had consumed from the kitchens, and had cleared the dishes after each course; Copplestone apparently had no other servants except for an aged cook. The servant must have been warned that the summons was imminent, for he immediately came in, carrying a large tray. On the tray was a wooden rack which held a series of test-tubes and glass-stoppered vials, and a large manilla envelope. These items the servant carefully placed in front of the professor—who was, of course, seated at the head of the table.

"These," said Copplestone, indicating the test-tubes, "are the various vision-enhancing drugs which were my raw materials. Here"—at this point he touched one of the sealed vials, which was marked out by a ring of red paint—"is the last and best of the many mixtures which I made from them. Needless to say, it is not a simple mixture, and the complex series of treatments to which I submitted the various compounds is carefully set out in a formula which I have placed in this envelope. As you have doubtless observed, my experiments have taken their toll of my health, and I fear that I may have done myself irreparable damage in the course of the expeditions which I intend to relate to you tonight. In order that my discoveries may be made available to other interested parties I will give the formula to my good friend the doctor, and I will gladly give the remainder of the compound to any one of you who might care to volunteer to follow where I have led, in order to prove that what I have to tell you has at least *some* truth in it. There is enough for a single moderate dose, similar to that which I employed in the second of the three dream-journeys which I will describe to you."

Copplestone gave the envelope to the doctor, in an appropriately ceremonious fashion. The doctor placed it dutifully in the inner pocket of his jacket.

"Perhaps, Doctor," the professor said, "You would be kind enough to tell the others what you observed while you have attended me these last few days.

Our attention shifted to the doctor, who coughed rather gruffly. "I can only tell them what I saw, Copplestone," he said. "Nothing else."

"Nothing else is required, I assure you," said Copplestone.

The doctor seemed uncomfortable, but he nodded his head. "I observed Professor Copplestone on three separate occasions," he said, awkwardly. "On each occasion, I watched him inject the drug whose remnant you see in that vial into his arm, and I did not leave him until its effects had worn off.

"After taking the drug, Copplestone fell into a deep sleep, which quickly gave way to an unusual form of coma. His heartbeat slowed down to some twenty-eight beats per minute and his body temperature fell by some twelve or fourteen degrees Fahrenheit. His body suffered a considerable but not-quite-consistent loss of weight amounting to slightly less or slightly more than three stones, although its dimensions were not altered commensurately."

"What a pity," Wilde murmured. "Copplestone might otherwise have hawked his discovery as a convenient cure for obesity."

The doctor spared him a brief frown, but continued doggedly: "This condition persisted for the same length of time—approximately three hours and ten minutes—on each occasion, even though the professor increased the dosage at each stage of the experiment. As the end of each period approached, the professor's body was subject to tremors, which increased considerably in violence over the course of the three experiments. On the third occasion I was fearfully anxious lest the convulsions should cause his heart to stop. When the professor regained consciousness he was noticeably weak, but his body did not recover all the weight which it had lost; the first coma resulted in a net loss of seven pounds, the second ten and the third sixteen. It would be unwise in the extreme, in my opinion, for the professor to attempt any further experiments along these lines—and I must say that anyone who is prepared to give serious consideration to Copplestone's invitation to continue this work must bear in mind that he might do himself considerable harm."

THE HUNGER AND ECSTASY OF VAMPIRES

The professor seemed quite unperturbed by this dark warning.

"Thank you," he said. Then, addressing the whole company again, he continued: "I will not bore you with a lengthy account of my preliminary experiments, nor with any elaborate presentation of my discoveries in organic chemistry, fascinating though they are. As to the nature of the mechanism involved in the process of precognition, even I can only speculate. However, it may be worth bearing in mind that although the locus of the individual mind is normally limited to the body at a particular moment in time, this does not mean that the mind has a particular *location* within the body. Sir William will, I think, bear me out when I say that there is now an abundance of evidence that the mind is capable of extending its function beyond the body, producing in the process what we normally call *apparitions?*"

The white-bearded man of science nodded his head. "The evidence for the survival of the mind after death, and its ability to formulate a fragile envelope for the purpose of earthly manifestation is now overwhelming," he agreed.

"Not all apparitions are vestiges of that post-mortem kind," said Copplestone, "as my story will demonstrate. The naturally-occurring compounds traditionally employed to induce visions are limited in scope, and the perceptions they permit are invariably distorted. However, such compounds do indeed allow the human mind to extend its perceptive range in both space and time. Space and time are, of course, merely two different aspects of the unitary fabric of the cosmos. Perception of any kind would be impossible without some kind of physical presence, so projections of this kind require the synthesis of a body of sorts, sometimes misleadingly called an *astral body*.

THE HUNGER AND ECSTASY OF VAMPIRES

"The compound which I eventually refined and perfected increased the powers of the natural compounds very considerably. The range of achievable projection was increased, and—perhaps more importantly—the degree of conscious control which I was able to exercise over my remote manifestation was very greatly enhanced. After a few preliminary experiments I was very eager to employ what I had begun to call my *time machine* in the exploration of the future of mankind."

"You don't care to tell us, I suppose," said the pale young man, rather rudely, "what will win the Derby this year?" He seemed curiously hostile, almost as though he had been insulted in some obscure fashion.

"Alas," said Copplestone, "my machine is so very powerful that it would require an impractical precision of dosage to travel sixty years, let alone six months, and I have reason to think that it would be impossible to remain in such a near future for more than a split second. In order to achieve a vision of reasonable coherency, and to take advantage of the conscious control which this compound allows, one must work in terms of thousands or tens of thousands of years."

"Not *hundreds* of thousands?" asked the young man, intemperately. Now that he was no longer schooling his speech so carefully his lower-class accent was discernible even to my untutored ears.

"The dosage required to journey so far might easily prove fatal," said Copplestone, whose equanimity was unconquerable by irony. "I did not dare to venture as far as *that*."

The young man scowled, and muttered something hardly audible, which may or may not have included the word *plagiarism*. His companion placed a soothing hand on his wrist, bidding him be patient and listen.

"My sketchy explanations have clearly strained your credulity too far, although my story has not yet even begun," said Copplestone, looking around at the uneasy faces which confronted him, "but I will press on regardless. Perhaps, though, some of you would also like to make preliminary statements about your opinions as to what I have said regarding the possible perceptibility of the future?"

I certainly did not, and felt uncomfortable to be asked, but some of my companions were not so shy.

"I don't believe in your damned native seers," said the American, brusquely, "and I don't believe in Sir William's apparitions either, although he's promised to show me a few while I'm here. But I believe in causality all right, and so I accept that *in principle* the future might be foreseen. Uncertainty is merely the consequence—the inevitable consequence, alas—of ignorance."

"*That* is surely certain," said the pale young man. "The future is determined, and hence potentially discoverable, at least to the extent that we can gather the relevant data. But..."

"I agree also," said his curly-haired companion, swiftly. "The origin of motion, which was the primal Act of Creation, already contained the plan of universal evolution."

"But what of free will?" asked the British scientist, seemingly impatient to disagree with the man he had invited to accompany him. "Men have the power to choose what they will do, and their choices determine the shape of their own futures. The future of mankind will be the sum of those choices, not the product of any merely mechanical laws. Consciousness is immune to the laws of causality which apply to inert objects. There *are* such things as premonitory dreams, but we should certainly consider the probability that they are warnings of what may happen, not glimpses of something immutable that *already exists*."

"I agree with Sir William, at least about the freedom of the will," said the doctor, gruffly. "Even if human beings are part of some unfolding plan, they have the power to alter it. The future of mankind depends entirely on the force and competence of the human will. We were not impelled here tonight by some irresistible force of necessity, and not one of us really doubts that he might be somewhere else entirely if it had pleased him to go."

"Neither Milton nor Mill could find a contradiction here," said Wilde, mildly. "Both would argue that our choices are real, and yet their outcomes would be known with perfect certainty to an omniscient mind. Yes, they would argue, we have the power of choice—but the choices we make are caused by our characters and interests, and are therefore predictable. Mill says that when our friends act unexpectedly we do not shrug our shoulders and attribute our surprise to the inevitable consequences of the freedom of the will—instead, he points out, we simply conclude that we did not know them as well as we thought and did not fully comprehend the causes of their actions."

I noticed that Wilde did not offer an opinion of his own, but was content with introducing the relevant ideas of others. I also noticed that the doctor's grey-eyed companion made no effort to intervene in the discussion, even when a momentary silence fell.

Dr. Copplestone turned to me, and said: "Do you have an opinion, Count?"

THE HUNGER AND ECSTASY OF VAMPIRES

"I have an opinion of sorts," I said, a little reluctantly. "I hold that there *is* an inescapable destiny that faces us all, and the universe itself. It is death. Perhaps we have the power to delay our course, or attain the end by different routes, but in the final analysis, there is no other fact, no other absolute."

I had always been a fatalist, and could not conceive that anything Copplestone might say would change my mind. How arrogant, how unimaginative and how wrong I was!

"Death is not the end," said the pillar of the Society for Psychical Research. "That is proven; we need not doubt it."

I saw the excitable young man shake his head vigorously, but for once he had discretion enough not to raise his reedy voice in protest. Copplestone lifted a placatory hand.

"Enough, gentlemen," he said. "Let us not fall to squabbling. When I have said what I have to say, you might be better informed to carry this argument forward—if you can believe my story."

"Is there any reason why we should not?" asked the American, ironically. He, at least, seemed fully prepared to disbelieve it.

"Only that it is incredible," said Copplestone, soberly. His tired eyes shone with reflected firelight, and he suddenly seemed to me to be extremely sad as well as debilitated—as if the world which had once been home to him had turned traitor, and cast him into some private hell of unbelonging. I felt an altogether unaccustomed pang of sympathy, and looked down at the wine in my glass, which had not the power to intoxicate me.

"If it were not incredible," said Wilde, pleasantly, "it would not be worth the ceremony. I am hoping for something very extraordinary indeed, and I trust that you will not

THE HUNGER AND ECSTASY OF VAMPIRES

disappoint us. As for myself, I am sufficiently realistic to be eager to believe anything, provided only that it is an obvious and grandiose lie."

Copplestone had the grace to smile at this, although it could not have been the kind of support he wanted. "In that case," he said, "I will proceed to describe the three expeditions which I undertook while the faithful doctor patiently stood guard over my *residuum*."

* * * *

4

"The first subjective sensation induced by the compound whose external effects the doctor has described," Copplestone explained, "is one of dizziness and disorientation. As the drug spreads through the bloodstream the mind is invaded by images of a bizarre and rather incoherent fashion. I am certain that if I could only train myself to concentrate upon a few elements of the torrent, thus making them selectively captive in the net of memory, useful information might be derived therefrom, but I have not so far managed to master the trick.

"After a time, however, the flood of inchoate images eases, and there is a process of settlement attended by a sensation of *coming together*, which corresponds with the formation of what I shall call, for want of a better word, a *timeshadow*. This is an actual, corporeal entity, visible to the inhabitants of the space and time in which it appears, but it is considerably less substantial than an ordinary body. My timeshadow was not sufficiently attenuated to pass through walls, although the much fainter shadow-selves projected by means of naturally-occurring drugs might be....but I ought perhaps to leave further discussion of that topic until I have described the manner in which I learned about the odd properties of my projected self.

THE HUNGER AND ECSTASY OF VAMPIRES

"I should explain in advance that the time which elapsed while the good doctor was standing watch over my unconscious body and the time experienced by my timeshadow did not run in parallel. A timeshadow's attenuation has a temporal as well as a physical aspect, which has the effect of stretching its subjective experience. An hour of real-body time corresponds to a longer period of timeshadow time, but the actual proportion varies somewhat according to the dosage—and hence, I think, in proportion to the time-difference involved. I was therefore present in the future world where my timeshadow coalesced for considerably longer than three hours.

"When the world about me first came into clear focus I found myself on a lightly-wooded hillside. The sun, which stood high in the sky, seemed identical to the one with which we are all familiar, but the trees were not the familiar trees of the English countryside. The green of their leaves was more vivid, and their smooth bark was lustrous, as though varnished. Their trunks were stout and very little gnarled. I could hear birdsong, but I caught only the most fleeting glimpses of the birds themselves as they fluttered from crown to crown, and could not easily compare them to the species I knew.

"I was surprised to find no trace whatsoever of the city of London, for I had assumed that I would remain in the same place while moving in time. Either that assumption was false, or I was so far displaced in time that all vestiges of the world's greatest city had been quite obliterated.

"Not without difficulty, I raised my hand to place it before my face. I half-expected that I might find it transparent, or at least translucent, but it was opaque, and lined in a familiar fashion. I looked down, and—somewhat to my surprise but

THE HUNGER AND ECSTASY OF VAMPIRES

greatly to my relief—found that I was not naked. I was not clad in the kind of suit in which I had left my true body, but I was wearing a thin white tunic and trousers. These were designed according to no model I had ever actually seen, and I could only assume that they were a minimal concession to my sense of modesty. This seemed to confirm what I believed about the ability of my own mind—without, apparently, any actual exertion of my conscious will—to interfere creatively with the sensory aspect of the drug's operation. This was not altogether good news. If a sense of propriety could alter the content of my prophetic vision, what might more powerful agents like fear and hope make manifest?

"The grass which grew to between ankle- and knee-height in the open between the trees was as vividly green as the foliage of the trees, and I could not help but reflect, ironically, that if this futuristic grass really were greener than the grass of the nineteenth century it must be a good omen—but I could not, of course, be certain that the difference was in the grass rather than in the sensory apparatus of my unusual corpus.

"There were a few coloured flower-heads raised above the grass, mostly blue or purple, and there were insects paying court to them: bee-like humming creatures and patterned butterflies. I did not pause, though, to study the insect-life of the period into which I had come—I wanted to seek out more interesting sights. From my vantage-point half way up the hill I could see a road, and in the distance a village, or perhaps the outskirts of a town. The road was very smooth and regular, as though it had been hewn from a single strip of soft stone, and the distant buildings seemed very clean in the bright sunlight, with roofs neatly tiled in brown and green, and walls mostly pale grey or pastel blue. There were no vehicles on the road but there were people walking in either direction, in pairs or small groups.

"When I tried to move down the hill I realised why it had required such an effort to raise my hand. A timeshadow may walk, run or jump like any other body, but the habits ingrained by ordinary experience must be modified. Although one might expect the opposite, a timeshadow seems to its tenant to be unusually heavy and rather sluggish. I found that what seemed to me, on the basis of ordinary experience, to be an effort adequate to take a step forward had to be considerably increased if I were to make headway, and that the headway I made was moderate—although, perhaps by way of compensation, once my timeshadow was in motion it had unusual momentum. My stride was slow, and required more than the usual thrust, but it was also long. My gait must have seemed very peculiar at first to the inhabitants of that future land, although I gradually learned to modify my actions to produce a less awkward result.

"I made my uncomfortable way down the hill. The people on the road must have caught sight of me, but no one stopped or turned to stare. It was not until I too was on the road that I was able to meet anyone's gaze or command attention.

"They were dressed even more simply than myself, each in a single garment not unlike a short nightshirt. I could hardly tell whether any one of them was male or female, although they differed in individual appearance as much as we do—given, at any rate, that not one showed the least sign of a beard. Most of them were conspicuously plump, and even the thinnest was certainly not slender by our standards.

THE HUNGER AND ECSTASY OF VAMPIRES

There were children among them, though none very young, but there was no one who showed any marked sign of old age.

"While I stood for a few moments upon the road, recovering my breath, twelve or fourteen people must have passed me by in one direction and nearly as many in the other. All of them glanced at me, but only a few looked me up and down or reacted to my presence. The children seemed most curious, and one or two of them pointed, and spoke to the adults with them. I could not understand the language they spoke, but its sounds seemed to me to be softly Oriental. Their hue was oriental too—not exactly that pale shade of brown which we misrepresent as 'yellow', for it was far too ruddy, but by no means white. The cast of their eyes was Caucasian, though. Their complexions seemed very ruddy, and I noticed that the blue tracery of veins on their bare forearms was very thick and outstanding.

"*Why are they so incurious?* I wondered. *They see me, but in spite of the fact that I am not at all like them, they find nothing remarkable about me. Why are they not as excited by my appearance as men of my world would be if a ghost were to walk down Oxford Street in broad daylight? Can it be possible that timeshadows are so familiar in this world as to constitute a trivial nuisance, best ignored?*

"I tried to raise my hand to bid a group of them to pause, but I was not yet master of my muscles and the gesture went wrong. Any thought of correcting it, however, was driven out of my mind when I tried to speak. My voice was very low indeed, and the words I was trying to form seemed exceedingly hoarse and hollow. At first, the syllables which I was attempting to string together ran into one another in a hopelessly inarticulate jumble.

THE HUNGER AND ECSTASY OF VAMPIRES

"The passers-by seemed rather more startled by my voice than by my appearance, but the effect on those I had been trying to interrupt was the opposite of what I had hoped. They speeded up, hurrying on their way, and others began to alter their courses so as to steer clear of me. When I stepped towards them they moved—much more gracefully—to increase the distance. I tried to protest, but it was futile. I could not blame them; had I heard another man speaking as I was, no matter that I could understand the language in which the words were, I would have taken him for a madman or a freak. It seemed sensible to hold my renegade tongue, at least for the time being.

"I began to walk along the road, heading—as the greater number of the natives were—towards the nearby village. My gait gradually became smoother as I went, and even at its worst did not alarm the indigenes as much as my distorted voice. Even so, they kept their distance, and were careful not to approach too close. They were by no means mortally afraid, but they were wary of me.

"I was soon among the buildings of the town—which did indeed seem to be a town, for once I was there I could see no further limit to it. It was laid out in a remarkably orderly fashion, its streets curving to follow the contours of the gentle slopes but otherwise very regular in their spacing. The houses differed slightly from one another in size and style, but the overall impression I got was one of astonishing uniformity. So far as architectural design was concerned the limits of variation were narrow, and there seemed to be an absolute uniformity of building technique. At close range I could see that the walls were made out of pale bricks supported and separated by thin layers of mortar, laid with awesomely mechanical regularity.

THE HUNGER AND ECSTASY OF VAMPIRES

The houses had glazed windows set in frames of some substance I had never encountered; these were all exactly the same size, as were the doors, which were constructed of the same substance as the window-frames.

"There seemed to be only one other kind of edifice apart from the houses, at least in this part of the town: every now and again I would pass a much larger construction, like a huge low barn, with numerous doors but no windows at all. I often saw people going into the houses or coming out of them, but in the course of that first stroll through the streets of the town I never saw anyone go into or come out of the windowless buildings.

"I suppose that I had always tacitly expected that the world of the future would be cleaner and more orderly than our own, and that life would have become less chaotic, if not entirely free of strife. I had expected, too, to find life more leisurely—but the image with which I was confronted now seemed to take all these things to a discomfiting extreme!

"As I looked about me at the people in the streets I could see hardly any real evidence of *purpose* in their movements. No one was in a hurry, and no one was carrying anything. None of the children had toys, and none seemed to be involved in the playing of any kind of game. Although they moved in groups, never as individuals, their conversations were dilatory. Members of one group never paused to exchange greetings or information with members of another. There were no vehicles to be seen, nor any domestic animals. The houses had no gardens.

"*This does not make sense*, I thought. *But if it is a fantasy conjured up by my mind and superimposed on a much richer reality, what on earth can my mind be about?*

THE HUNGER AND ECSTASY OF VAMPIRES

Why should it deprive the society of the future of all its verve and intelligence?

"I paused as I passed some of the windows and peered into the houses. I saw laden tables, and chairs drawn up around them, sometimes occupied and sometimes not, but I never saw anyone engaged in any activity except serving or eating food. I saw unfamiliar fruits being eaten with the fingers, and I saw people using spoons to draw various different liquids or solids from bowls, but I never saw a knife or a fork, or a plate. Everything was simple; life here seemed as carefully minimal as my clothing.

"The inner walls of the houses were as plain as the outer ones. I saw no pictures or hangings, nor any other kind of ornamentation. I saw no books or shelves. I saw cribs containing babies, and sometimes heard the babies wailing, but I could detect no signs of distress among the children who were old enough to walk.

"If the people inside a house became aware that I was looking in they would look back, evincing the same signs of mild alarm that the people on the road had showed when I tried to make contact with them, but they never tried to shoo me away, and did not seem overly offended by my invasion of their privacy. No one came to investigate my presence, even though it must have been obvious to everyone who saw me that I was not merely a stranger but an alien.

"At first I had thought the town rather pleasant because it was so neat and clean, but it quickly came to seem direly uncanny. The impression which grew upon me was of one of those miniature towns which are sometimes constructed as toys for the children of the very rich, where everything is present, but dramatically simplified.

THE HUNGER AND ECSTASY OF VAMPIRES

"*This is not human life*, I thought, *it is a mere simulation of it. These are not people, but imitations of people: automata of some kind, which can maintain some pretence of walking and talking, of eating, and perhaps excreting, but cannot do these things in any authentic sense.*

"I gave serious consideration to the hypothesis that all this might be nothing but an illusion conjured up by a sadly jejune imagination, but when I looked at the slowly-setting sun, and the display of colour it created by its effects upon the slightly-humid atmosphere, I could not believe that this was other than an actual world. The breeze, hardly perceptible in any case, felt odd upon my attenuated flesh, and I could not tell whether the dearth of scents was likewise an illusion of dull sensation, but when I recalled the hillside where so many natural things had deployed themselves in such a natural fashion, I could not help but starkly contrast the lifelessness of this crude forgery of human existence.

"Eventually, I became bolder, and I went into one of the houses, having first peered in through the windows. The people who lived there were seated at the table, enjoying a meal—and I do mean *enjoying*, for they seemed to relish what they were eating until I arrived. When I came into the room they stopped immediately, and got up. They were so obviously disconcerted by my invasion that I almost expected them to fall upon me and throw me out, but they did not. Instead they twittered at one another in their strange language, and backed up against the wall. The adults extended their arms protectively to the children.

"When I had come far enough away from the door the people of the house moved towards it—sidling rather than dashing—and went out, leaving me alone with their half-finished repast. In my attenuated form I was not sure that I could taste food properly, and I had not the slightest hunger or thirst, so I contented myself with inspecting the contents of the bowls by eye. Considering that everything else was so simple, the diet which these people enjoyed seemed unusually rich and varied. But where, I wondered, were the fields and orchards which generated this produce? Where were the markets in which it was traded? How was it brought into the houses?

"The inhabitants of the house had gone out into the street, and I watched them through the window to see if they would call for help. They did not. They waited, and they watched. They talked to one another, but not to other passersby.

"I went to investigate the other rooms in the house. There were several rooms upstairs, each containing a low bed and a closet in which half a dozen tunics hung. There was a bathroom downstairs, and a separate water-closet with a flushing toilet. The pipes which carried the water were not metallic and I could see no joints of the kind which might have required a plumber's attention. The taps in the bathroom were mere levers, and I could not open the cistern of the flushing toilet to see what kind of ballcock it contained.

"The kitchen had a sink too, but it had no range, no fireplace, no kettle, and no boiler. Hot water ran from one of the taps but I could see no apparatus for heating it. There were cupboards for bowls, spoons and some foodstuffs, but no utensils which might have been used in its preparation. There were, however, no less than three dumb-waiters whose shafts disappeared downwards into impenetrable depths—a fact which seemed all the more remarkable when I concluded, after assiduous searching, that the house had no basement or cellar that could be reached from the ground floor.

"*It is all mere surface, I thought. This whole town is but a toy, whose appearances are controlled from below by hidden mechanisms. But if it is all artifice, who or what can the artificers possibly be?*

"That was the question which preoccupied my mind as I went out into the gathering dusk, to see the last few fugitive rays of the setting sun as it sank beneath the coloured horizon, leaving the world to blue-grey twilight."

* * * *

5

As Copplestone paused I glanced at Wilde, whose lips were pursed in annoyance.

"These are not the brave and gaudy lies I hoped to hear," he whispered, although we had to lean back to either side of the American scientist's chair in order to maintain the privacy of the observation. "They are rather anaemic—so very unelaborate in their imagery as to be unworthy even of a professor."

I smiled thinly. "I could have hoped for a more exciting future," I admitted. "But it has the ring of sincerity, has it not? Perhaps we should not judge until we have have heard the unravelling of the mystery."

Wilde shrugged. "I suppose it would be churlish to condemn a puzzle before its solution is reported."

"Depends what kind of puzzle it is," muttered the mustachioed man of science. "Not much spark in this one, so far. No spark, no power—that's my experience."

Copplestone gave no indication that he was aware of our whispered comments. He had already resumed his narrative. "I had half-expected that nightfall would put an end to activity within the town," he went on. "Just as our children

THE HUNGER AND ECSTASY OF VAMPIRES

must put away their dolls' houses when the day is done, so it seemed appropriate that the mysterious owners of this sham of life might put their charges to bed, and leave their habitat to silence and inaction. I was quite wrong. The family whose home I had invaded made no attempt to reclaim their territory as the twilight faded, and I observed that many more people were emerging on to the streets. Soon there was assembled a far greater throng than I had seen in mid-afternoon.

"Darkness did not fall. As the sky became black and the stars began to shine through, the streets lit up. I do not mean that lamps were lit; it was the actual fabric of the roadway which began to glow with a white, cold luminosity. I could see a similar light within some of the windows of the houses, but the lighted windows faded away as their inhabitants came out to join the gathering crowds in the street. I guessed that some surface within each room—a wall or the ceiling—must be made of some material similar to that of the roadway, and that there was some kind of control mechanism which ensured that light was released only when someone was actually in the room. I inferred that the light was a kind of artificial phosphorescence, or possibly a domestic bioluminescence akin to that which one sometimes sees faintly glimmering upon the surface of the sea.

"A half-moon had recently risen above the eastern horizon, and was slowly climbing higher. I studied its face closely, and was oddly relieved to find it quite unchanged. However many thousands of years had passed since the era of my birth, some things had evidently remained constant and inviolable.

"As the people in my immediate vicinity began to move past me, it seemed that for the first time they moved with a *purpose*. All those nearby were moving in the same direction, as though they had a common destination. Lit from below as they were, their marching figures seemed rather eerie, but curiosity impelled me to fall into step without delay, following those who moved ahead of me.

"I did not have far to go. I soon perceived that the crowd was heading for the nearest of those larger buildings with which the houses were interspersed. As I approached, I saw that all of its many doors now stood open, and that an orderly queue of people was forming at each one. I suppose that I could have barged ahead, but it seemed impolite to do so—and in any case, the queues were moving with reasonably rapidity. I simply took a place in one of them and waited for those in front to enter.

"In the meantime, I studied the people. As on the road, I could see no very young children, and no old people. The babies I had glimpsed in one or two of the houses had not been brought out. There was no talking in the lines, although people who arrived in groups always joined the same queue. My presence caused not the slightest disturbance even to the man who was directly in front of me or the woman who was directly behind. There was no hurry; patience ruled supreme.

"The light inside the barn-like building was as wan and white as that which illuminated the roadway, but it shone down from the ceiling and cast its shadows in what seemed to me to be a more ordinary way. There were plenty of shadows to be cast, for the building was crowded with machinery of some kind, much of which loomed up to a height considerably above that of a man. The vast room reverberated with a low humming sound, but there was no whining as of turning wheels, no clattering as of pistons and no hissing as of steam engines.

THE HUNGER AND ECSTASY OF VAMPIRES

It was, I guessed, an *electrical* hum, and I concluded that the whole town must run on electrical power generated in some subterranean region. I resolved to look closely at the machinery so that I would be able to describe it minutely to someone like Sir William or Mr. Tesla, but I fear that I was unable at the time to make the most of that resolution, for reasons which will shortly become apparent.

"The queues, which remained as orderly within the building as without, extended into narrow corridors between the hulking masses, there vanishing from my sight. I stayed in my place, more fascinated for the moment by the machinery than the people. I could see that there were glass-faced dials set in the sides of the machines at eye-level, and levers and switches positioned as though for the human arm, but no one made any attempt to read the indicators or activate the levers.

"There was a slight pulse in the floor beneath my feet, which implied that there was indeed more machinery at a lower level, and I could see steps leading down at various positions along the inner wall of the building. There were also upward flights of steps made out of what looked like wrought iron, which led to catwalks that ran all around the inner walls. These were connected by a sparse webwork of railed walkways, which bridged the gap between the longer sides of the rectangular space.

"Distributed about these catwalks, leaning casually on the guard-rails, were a dozen human figures, distributed in groups of two or three. As soon as I caught sight of them they commanded my attention. For the first time I thought: *Here are real people at last. Here are the masters of this vast charade.*

"From where I stood the men on the walkways were mere silhouettes, limned against the evenly-lit ceiling, and I

THE HUNGER AND ECSTASY OF VAMPIRES

could not hear a word of their conversation. Nevertheless, I had not the slightest doubt that they were not of the same kind as the docile cattle which swarmed around me. Their postures were lazy, their attitudes too obviously negligent for them to be anything other than people engaged in a desultory fight against boredom. They were evidently in charge of whatever was happening here, and yet their presence was hardly necessary; the whole process was working automatically, at least for the time being.

"I was tempted to step out of line and go to one of the flights of steps, in order that I might ascend and try to make contact with the *real* inhabitants of this strange future world, but I hesitated. The line in which I had taken my place had now progressed so far that I was on the point of entering the narrow corridor between the ranks of machines. I knew that in a minute or two I would be able to see where the queue was heading, and what the people in it had come to do. I decided that there would be time enough to go upstairs when I had satisfied my curiosity on *that* point.

"The narrow corridor extended for about forty yards between two rows of compartments or stalls. Every few seconds someone would emerge from one or other of these stalls and the person at the head of the queue would go forward to take their place. Each stall was occupied for several minutes at a time, but there were so many of them that the queue was kept moving at a moderate pace. When the man ahead of me moved—as chance would have it, into the first space on the left—I did not stand patiently by waiting for my own turn. I went with him, to watch what he did.

"Within the dimly-lit compartment there was an outward-facing chair, on which the man sat down. He could

THE HUNGER AND ECSTASY OF VAMPIRES

see that I was standing before him, watching him, and he hesitated momentarily, but the inhibiting effect of my presence was insufficient to deflect him from his purpose. He reached behind him to pull something from the wall.

"As he pulled, a long tube of what looked like transparent rubber was drawn through an aperture; on the end of it, which he had gripped, was a metal device which was headed by a slender needle and from which dangled a number of threads. Hitching up the skirt of his brief tunic, the man casually thrust the point of the needle into the flesh inside his thigh, and with practised ease he distributed the threads so that they adhered to his skin and held the needle in place. He then pressed a small switch set in the wall behind him, and sat back listlessly. He did not bother to watch the blood which rapidly filled the transparent tube and disappeared into the wall behind him.

"I can hardly convey the horror which began to grow in me as I watched all this happening. The bovine nonchalance of it all was quite chilling.

"Another stall became vacant further down the line, and I squeezed myself further into the compartment in order to let the woman who had been standing behind me in the queue move past. She showed no disinclination to do so, nor any resentment of my failure to take my turn. The man—to whom I was now standing very close indeed—looked up at me with an expression I could not evaluate. It did not seem like anxiety or loathing, but I had lost confidence in my ability to make such ready judgments of people who were clearly far more alien than I had assumed.

"As my horror increased I began to see new significance in the fact that all the townspeople seemed so plump and so full-complexioned, and so curiously docile. It burst upon me with all the force of a revelation that this barn-like edifice was indeed a barn, and that these humans I had likened in my mind to cattle were exactly that: domesticated creatures of little intelligence and less independence, who came to be 'milked' at dusk instead of dawn, giving a copious yield of the good red blood which they had been selectively bred to produce superabundantly.

"I understood, belatedly, that the 'houses' in which these 'people' lived were not really houses at all, but merely animal-shelters, whose plumbing and heating had perforce to be controlled from elsewhere, by the herdsmen who kept such livestock.

"*They are vampires!* I thought, with an awful thrill of superstitious dread. *The masters of this world are vampires, which feed on human blood. Nor are they predators which covertly haunt the night, but careful farmers. They have enslaved mankind and reduced the human species to a status hardly above that of the goats and sheep which the earliest human nomads kept.*"

* * * *

6

Copplestone paused again, briefly, as the memory of what he had experienced—or, rather, dreamt—made him shudder. I could see sweat standing on his brow, and his colour had grown worse. I wondered whether he had enough strength to reach the end of his story—and I wondered, too, whether I had the stomach to hear him out.

I had not expected anything like this. Wilde's passing mention of the name of one of Vambery's English acquaintances as a potential member of the audience had awakened my concern but had not informed me that there might be some danger of embarrassment were I to come in his stead.

I dare say that for a moment or two my own colour was as unprepossessing, in its own way, as Copplestone's. I must have been as white as a sheet, and it was all I could do to keep myself from trembling with wrath. Had all this, I could not help but wonder, been set up expressly for my discomfort? Was it all a drama planned to taunt and threaten me?

A few moments of careful reflection assured me, however, that I was being oversensitive. There was no connection whatever between the kind of fantasy that

Copplestone was spinning out and the rumours that Vambery had spread save for the use of the word *vampire*. I reminded myself that it was a common notion nowadays, frequently employed in literature and shallow conversation. Science had not killed off the old folktales popularised by Dom Augustine Calmet and his inquisitive kin; it had merely served to make them seem quaint, and therefore interesting.

I looked around at my companions, to satisfy myself that there was no one seated at the table who could possibly believe in vampires. The only pang of doubt I had was when I met the eyes of the man sitting opposite my station: the doctor's eccentric friend. He was looking at me with a most peculiar expression.

He has been ill, I reminded myself. *He is an opium-eater of sorts, and prey to delusions. It would not matter what he thought, if he thought anything untoward at all.*

I was able to meet his stare quite frankly, although it did not seem that my openness set his troubled mind at rest.

"As I realised what was happening," Copplestone continued, "I shrank back against the partition which separated the cubicle from the next in line. My sudden timorousness was not the result of anything the creature with which I shared it had done, but rather because it had occurred to me to wonder what might happen if the watchers on the catwalk overcame their burden of tedium sufficiently to notice that I was there.

"I looked up hastily to see how many of the silhouetted figures were visible from where I stood, and realised that I was shielded by the surrounding walls from all but two of them, who were positioned on a bridge some sixty feet away, at an angle of thirty degrees or so. They were facing the other direction, and I realised as I became calmer again that it would not have been so very easy for them to catch sight of me had they been looking my way, unless they had unusually sharp eyes. Save for my head and shoulders I was completely hidden from their view, and because the diffuse light was above them the entire floor area must have been rather gloomy. Even so, I began making plans as to how best I might make my exit from the building unseen.

"My earlier enthusiasm to make contact with these masters had evaporated now that I knew that they kept other human beings as livestock. Perhaps this was cowardly of me, but the sudden rush of terrible enlightenment which I had experienced had come as quite a shock. I did not know what to do.

"The man in the chair began again to address his attentions to the device attached to his leg. He detached the adhesive strips, withdrew the needle, and held it carefully while it was drawn back into the wall. He took a piece of lint from a dispenser and used it to mop up the bead of blood which formed upon his thigh, discarding it into a repository set low down in the wall. He seemed to be glad that the time had come for him to be gone, but that might have been a result of my presence rather than the kind of relief which might follow the conclusion of a painful ordeal.

"As another came to take his place I was pleased to slide myself out of the way so as to offer no obstruction. This one was a girl, seemingly no more than ten years old—one of the youngest I had seen in the queues. I had no wish to distress her with my presence, nor to watch her making her donation of blood. I began to walk down the corridor in the direction that all those went who had performed their function.

"I felt sure that all I had to do was to follow the others, and behave exactly as they did, so that anyone who caught sight of me from above would not see that I was not one of them. It seemed easy enough. At the far end of the corridor there was an open space much like the one from which I had come, but somewhat narrower and far less crowded—for there were, of course, no queues here. The nearest door was only fifteen paces away, but so was the nearest ascending staircase, *and standing on the seventh step of that stairway, looking down at the people who had done their duty and were going home, was a lone man clad in black.*

"Immediately after catching sight of him I attempted to step back into the corridor, to hide myself behind the angle of the wall, but it was too late; as soon as I had seen him, he had seen me—and at this range he could be in no doubt that I was different from the rest. The absurd clothing which my scrupulous psyche had seen fit to invent for the sake of my modesty was enough to mark me out instantly, and my height, thinness and colouring would surely have been enough even if I had contrived to conjure up a tunic of exactly the kind the human cattle wore.

"The man in black was not brightly-lit, and I could not make out his features very well, but the way his body shifted made it apparent that he was by no means as incurious as the people I had tried to speak to on the road. This was a thinking being, but I had every reason to believe that he was no more like me than those who had come here to be milked of their blood.

However human his form might be, I thought, *he is a monster.*

"I know well enough now that it was entirely the wrong thing to do, but panic took over. I could not escape by turning around and running back along the corridor, because there was too far to go and little hope of unimpeded progress, and I certainly did not want to emerge at the other end with more of the black-clad watchers waiting patiently to catch me. I ran forwards, taking a course diagonally away from the stairway where the watcher stood, towards one of the open doors which allowed the human cattle egress from the building.

"I had not practised running, and the moment I began to move in a new way all my former awkwardness returned in full measure. My body felt heavy, more lumpen and leaden than before, and it seemed to me that the strides I was taking were very slow and very painful. The confusion of these alien sensations served only to amplify my panic, but the more effort I exerted to hurl myself forward the more ungainly I seemed to become.

"I felt myself begin to fall, and experienced a sharp thrill of terror as I realised that my reflexes were incapable of compensating. I could not regain my balance.

"The impact which I suffered as I met the floor jarred me, but did not knock me out, and I scrambled to regain my feet. By the time I had done so, however, the man from whom I fled had come down from the stair and was moving swiftly towards me.

"I could see his face more clearly now, and I could see that it was even paler than my own, save only for the lips, which seemed red and full. His eyes were peculiar, with a hint of luminous green about them; they at least seemed manifestly inhuman.

"I lurched unsteadily towards the door, but I could not have reached it had not my pursuer been impeded. As it

THE HUNGER AND ECSTASY OF VAMPIRES

happened, his path crossed that of a woman who had emerged from the corridor to his left. She walked dazedly in front of him and they collided. She let out a wail of anguish as she realised, too late, what had happened. He tripped, and fell as heavily as I had, howling as he hit the floor.

"Desperation lent me the skill which I needed, and I managed to accelerate my progress towards the doorway. I hurled myself through it just ahead of another of the cattle-men.

"It was not until the cooler air struck my face that it occurred me to wonder what to do next. Where could I run to? Where could I hide? The urgency of these questions over-rode any sober consideration of the degree of danger I was in. I firmly believed, on the basis of a very plausible intuition, that if anything happened which fatally wounded the attenuated body which currently housed my consciousness, that I would really die, and would lose my chance of slipping back through time into my own body.

"I stumbled away from the doorway, determined to reach the shadows beyond the illuminated strip of roadway, which seemed to offer shelter of a kind—but even as I did so I realised that the dull humming sound which had filled the huge shed had not given way to the gentle silence which had reigned out here before I entered the building. Far from it; the night was now filled with sound, which came from above rather than below.

"Having taken no more than three or four steps into the darkness beside the roadway I looked up into the starry sky, and saw to my astonishment that it was full of shadows, *as if a great flock of huge and monstrous bats were wheeling above the town.*

"For a moment, I thought the flying things really were predatory haunters of the night, but they were not alive. They carried lights to signal their position to one another, and their wings were rigid. It was impossible to make out their exact shapes, although they were no more than a few hundred feet above the ground, but the thrumming noise of their engines was unmistakably similar to the sound which had filled the huge barn. They were machines.

"The sky was so full of stars that their temporary occlusion was both obvious and disconcerting, but I perceived that the machines were not as numerous as I had first thought. There were dozens rather than hundreds, but even dozens seemed astonishing and alarming.

"*In God's name*, I thought, *what mad kind of world is it into which I have been delivered?*

"Sheer confusion must have brought me to a standstill, for I was no longer running. I was impotently staring upwards into the sky when rough hands grabbed me from behind.

"I heard voices exclaiming, and although I could not understand a word of their language I was sure that I could read frank amazement in their tone. I found time to wonder what it felt like for them when mortal men—if these were, indeed, mortal men—took hold of my attenuated form. Now that my flight had ended, panic had lost its tyranny over my processes of thought, and as I was dragged back towards the doorway through which I had come I felt perversely free to delight in contemplation of the puzzle I might pose to my captors."

* * * *

7

Copplestone seemed anything but delighted as he spoke these words, and his voice dissolved into a fit of coughing. The doctor got up from his seat and rushed to his side. The professor's trembling now grew worse, and it seemed that he was on the brink of some kind of fit, but he grew calmer again as the coughing faded.

After a brief lapse of time the doctor suggested that the rest of us should move from the dining-room into the smoking-room, while he saw to the needs of his patient. He promised that the story would continue as soon as Copplestone was fit enough to tell it.

As we rose from the table and moved to do as we were bid Wilde was engaged in conversation by the American, and I found myself moving to the door alongside one of the two young men. It was the one who had seemed—and still seemed—to be rather agitated.

"You do not seem to be enjoying yourself," I remarked, as I stood side to let him precede me. He looked at me with perverse annoyance, as though my politeness might somehow constitute a veiled insult, but he obviously thought better of his suspicion.

THE HUNGER AND ECSTASY OF VAMPIRES

"I beg your pardon," he said, in his awkwardly-distinctive voice. "I am confused. I must confess that this whole evening has the appearance of being a joke at my expense."

I was slightly startled, in that I was still wondering whether Copplestone's story might be an elaborate joke at *my* expense.

"How so?" I asked.

"Do you read the *National Observer?*" he asked.

"I fear not," I replied, making no real effort to sound apologetic.

"I suspect that Copplestone does. I suspect that he has been an avid reader of a series of articles which I contributed to the journal, couched in the form of a story told by a time-traveller to a group of his acquaintances, concerning his exploration of future time. And yet....he showed no sign that he recognised my name when Shiel introduced me, and Shiel assures me that Copplestone could not possibly have guessed that he would invite me to be his guest. The professor certainly cannot know—unless, perchance, he is intimate with Henley—that I have already rewritten the articles into a form more akin to a novel, for serialization in *The New Review*. But what is the purpose of this apparent plagiarism? I cannot fathom it."

Nor could I. "Perhaps you are a trifle over-sensitive," I suggested. "Are the resemblances between your story and his really so close that there is no possibility of coincidence?"

"They are," he said, positively. "It is true that my time-traveller uses an actual machine to transport him into the future rather than a drug, but that makes it all the more significant that Copplestone uses the term 'time machine', which I have adopted into the title of the newest version of my story. What my protagonist discovers in the first future era he visits is so similar to what Copplestone has described as to be an evident copy."

I found this news strangely disturbing. To find one story-teller dabbling in nightmares of this particular kind was puzzling; to find two was positively uncanny. "You have also foreseen a future in which the human race serves as the cattle of a race of vampires?" I said.

He blinked in perplexity. "Oh no," he said. "Not *vampires*, as such. But the difference is inconsiderable. In my vision of the year 802,701 the human race has divided into two separate species. One of them—the Eloi—lives meekly upon the surface, enjoying a life of ease, while the other—the Morlocks—lives underground, tending the machinery which sustains the apparent Golden Age. They are, you see, the ultimate descendants of the two great classes of our society: the leisured and the labourers. But in my story, the wretched and ugly Morlocks have their revenge upon the lovely Eloi, for they emerge from their caverns by night to prey upon their one-time masters, feeding upon their flesh. You see, sir, that Copplestone's story is merely a simple transfiguration of mine; it is plagiarism pure and simple. There is no other possible explanation."

"Pardon me," interposed another voice, "but I believe there is."

We both turned, neither of us having realised until that moment that anyone else was listening to our conversation. It was the older of the two men of science: the white-bearded Briton.

"I should be interested to hear it," I murmured, when the young man merely gaped.

THE HUNGER AND ECSTASY OF VAMPIRES

"Even sceptics like my friend Tesla must admit," said the old man, equably, "that it is at least *possible* that all men are capable of a degree of precognition. Many men of science accept that there is good evidence that our dreams routinely bring us news of the future—which is admittedly confused by our own minds with other materials. Must we not admit the possibility that *you*, Mr. Wells, have something of the innate ability which the best of Copplestone's native shamans possess, and that your mind is capable of reaching into the future even without the kind of chemical assistance which Copplestone requires. You, not unnaturally, construe your vision as a pure product of your own imagination—a story which you have invented, shaped and polished—but perhaps it is a true, if somewhat blurred, vision of the shape of things to come. Perhaps, sir, you are a modern Sibyl, and the story you have written is the produce of the contemporary Delphic Oracle: an authentic prophecy, differing only in the idiosyncratic literary details which you have used for its embellishment, from Copplestone's equally authentic vision."

It was difficult to judge from the man's tone how serious he was. He spoke lightly, as though he were elaborating a hypothesis rather an stating a belief, and there was a hint of gentle flattery about the way he offered the young man the opportunity to pass himself off as a man more gifted than others of his kind. The young man seemed to me exactly the type to nurse such delusions of grandeur, but his response to the argument was conscientiously sceptical.

"That is every bit as fantastic as Dr Copplestone's story, Sir William!" he exclaimed.

"Which is," the old man pointed out, "every bit as fantastic as your own."

THE HUNGER AND ECSTASY OF VAMPIRES

"But mine is pure invention!"

"If what you said earlier about the future being determined and discoverable is true," I murmured, playing Devil's Advocate, "there may be no such thing as *pure invention*. If everything has a cause, then who is to say whether the similarity between Copplestone's story and yours arises because yours is the cause of his, or because both have a cause in common?"

"If what I said about the future being determined is true," the young man retorted, "all causes must be prior to their consequences. If the future can influence the present, the logic of the argument is trapped by a vicious circularity."

At that moment, Professor Copplestone re-entered the room, seemingly revived and revitalized by whatever treatment the doctor had administered. He suggested to us that we take the seats which had been set out for us around the fireplace.

As dutiful guests, young Mr. Wells, Sir William and I had no option but to postpone our argument while our host resumed his tale.

* * * *

8

"I was carried by my captors into a curious Underworld," Copplestone reported, a little hoarsely. "It was illuminated, apparently by the same method that the houses were illuminated, but not so brightly. The light had an odd hue, somewhere between blue and violet. I suppose that there was as much light as there is on a clear night when the moon is full, but its peculiar colour made it seem altogether alien. My own eyes adapted well enough, when a few minutes had passed, to allow me to see what was around me, but I understood that eyes for which that level of light was optimal must be quite different from mine.

"It was futile to struggle against the strong arms which held me, for it was obvious that however heavy my limbs felt to me, I was not much of a burden to my captors. They held me very gingerly, as though my insubstantial body felt strange and unpleasant, but there was no prospect of my breaking away, and now that I knew that they were not bent on my immediate destruction I began to think more clearly again. I realised that if I were to come to a fuller understanding of this world then I would have to descend into the Underworld, to see what manner of men dwelt there and what kind of existence they maintained.

THE HUNGER AND ECSTASY OF VAMPIRES

"While I was taken down the stairs I tried to inspect my captors more closely. As my sight became clearer I confirmed my earlier impression that they were very pale of face, and that their eyes glowed faintly green. I saw now, though, that these eyes were very much like cat's eyes, with lenticular pupils. They had full lips, which seemed nearly black rather than red. They were all male but all beardless, and their faces were curiously unblemished; it was impossible to guess how old they might be. Their dark clothing was more elaborate than that worn by the people of the town, but simpler than the conventional suits of our own era.

"They took me down two more flights of stairs, with a winding corridor in between, and then through a further maze. I knew that I would not be able to find my way back again, but I had recovered control of my emotions by now and I was far less afraid than I had been. I reminded myself that my time in this world was strictly limited, and that I was certain to return to my body in due course. From the viewpoint of my captors I would simply vanish into thin air. In the meantime, the task before me was to find out as much as I possibly could about the vampires and their empire of the night.

"On the other hand, I remained sharply aware of the probability that I could be permanently injured by any violence which they chose to do to my attenuated body. I decided that I must oblige my captors as far as I was able, so as to encourage them to handle me kindly. Fortunately, they seemed to have no intention of causing me pain, at least for the time being. When I ceased to struggle they ceased to treat me so rigorously, and by the time we arrived at our destination I was virtually walking alongside them, with their hands guiding me.

THE HUNGER AND ECSTASY OF VAMPIRES

"They took me into an extraordinary room, whose walls were mounted with numerous rectangular screens. Most of these screens were inert but four of them were active, displaying moving pictures of various kinds. I could make no sense of two of the images, which were diagrammatic, with associated printed text of a kind I could not decipher, but the other two were pictorial. One showed several persons in conversation—not people like those I had seen in the town, but beings like those who had seized me—while the other showed machines in flight: not huge airships like those which are so often described in popular fiction, but contraptions like those I had briefly seen outside, far more akin to rigid-winged birds or bats.

"Beneath the screens there were complicated panels decked with countless buttons and switches. I would dearly have loved to make sense of all this apparatus, but there was simply too much. It bore some faint resemblance to the cab of a railway locomotive or the bridge of a steamship, but I could not imagine how any human being could cope with the sheer profusion of it all.

"There were three persons already in the room, and when I was brought in they became very excited; the two who had been seated instantly stood up. They fired questions at my captors while they moved around me, inspecting me very curiously. They also attempted to fire questions at me, but I could not understand their language and my attempts to reply sounded grotesque even to me because of the hollow laboriousness of my pronunciation. I realised, numbly, that they had difficulty believing in me. They prodded and poked me in a manner which suggested that they doubted their own senses. They seemed astonished by my speech, perhaps as

THE HUNGER AND ECSTASY OF VAMPIRES

much by the curious distortion which afflicted my voice as by the unfamiliarity of my language, although they were probably not aware that I would have sounded quite different had it not been for the distorting effects of my attenuation.

"After several minutes of animated discussion their attitude changed. Solicitously, and with much ceremony, they ushered me to a chair situated before one of the screens, and invited me with a mime of exaggerated politeness to sit down. When I had done so, clumsily, one of them began moving his fingers over the control-panel before me, with incredible speed and dexterity.

"The image of yet another cat-eyed person appeared on the screen, and it was clear from his attitude that my image must have been simultaneously relayed to him. A voice which I assumed to be his emerged from a disc beneath the screen. There was a long and rather confused exchange of staccato conversation between the person on the screen and the persons clustering about me. One of my captors began signalling to me furiously, gesturing with his hand in front of his mouth. I inferred that he wanted me to speak, and I did so, haltingly at first but more fluently as he encouraged me to continue. In the meantime, two others left the room.

"I am not sure exactly what I said. I told them that my name was Copplestone, and repeated the syllables for emphasis, pointing at my chest in order to make their meaning clear. I then tried to give some account of the experiment which had brought me here—although I knew well enough that I might just as well have been reciting nursery rhymes for all the good it might do. If I hesitated, my interrogator-in-chief resumed his urgent signing, so I knew that they wanted me to keep talking whether they understood me or not.

"Just as I had earlier mastered the art of walking by dint of practising, so my speech improved by degrees. Within a few minutes I was enunciating clearly enough, although my voice still sounded unreasonably deep and slow. By that time I had little more to say about myself, but every time I faltered I was urged to continue. I could not quite bear to revert to nursery rhymes, so I began quoting verse—snippets of Shakespeare, Shelley and Tennyson. That seemed to suffice for their purpose, and after some twelve or fifteen minutes the one who had taken charge held up his hand to give me permission to stop. He then began playing with the control-board again, displaying once more that incredible dexterity.

"After a few moments, I heard the sound of my own voice emerging from the speaker from which the voice of the man on the screen had earlier emerged. I recognised words which I had earlier spoken, and winced at their uncouth tones. Embarrassment left me little space to wonder at the fact that my words had been so accurately recorded—and any wonderment I might have felt would have been banished entirely when the recording was interrupted by another voice, which said, as nearly as I can reproduce the words: 'Anglish. Is Anglish.'

"I looked up at the image of the man on the screen, but he was not speaking. Like me, he was listening—but he was looking at me eagerly, avid for some response. The voice which had spoken was as hollow and hoarse and distorted as mine, but that was presumably mere imitation.

"The one who had appointed himself my principal interlocutor gestured once again, demanding that I speak, and

I presumed that he wanted some confirmation of the identification. 'English,' I said, trying to correct the pronunciation. 'The language is *English*.'

"The words were immediately repeated back to me, adjusted so that they reflected exactly the syllables I had spoken. The voice, I now realised, was a calculated echo of my own, presumably produced by a machine which, with the resources I had provided, had contrived to identify the language which I spoke. That was the moment when it finally came home to me what resources these people had—and gave me to wonder whether they were, indeed, people at all, or whether they were creatures from some other world which had conquered, subdued and made prey of mankind.

"'Can you understand me?' I said, hesitantly. 'Do you know what I am saying?'

"There was no immediate reply. Instead, the speaker let loose a rapid burst of the alien tongue which my captors spoke, and I judged from their reaction—part astonishment, part delight—that it was a translation of what I had said. Then the man on the screen spoke, and there was a brief pause before what I assume to be a translation of *his* words emerged in English from the speaker: 'We understand. Your language is preserved in the memory banks. How did you come here? What manner of being are you?'

"I gathered from this that the information which I had given earlier had simply been used for the purpose of identifying the language which I spoke; presumably they could recover the recording at a later time, but in the meantime it might be simpler to respond to their questions. The ensuing conversation was unusually cumbersome because of the delays involved in the mechanical translation, and there were several hitches caused by mistranslation, but I will try to reproduce the bare essentials of it.

"'My name is Copplestone,' I said. 'I am a timeshadow. My own body lies unconscious....'" I intended to say *in the city of London, in the year 1895*, but I was not allowed to finish my sentence. This may have been a stroke of good luck, although I did not realise it at the time.

"'What is *timeshadow?*' demanded the machine, sharply. 'Explain!'

"'I am a man of the past,' I said. 'Your world is my future; this *timeshadow*—the strangely attenuated body which I present to your senses— is the means by which I can look into it.'

"This was translated, but the person on the screen seemed deeply confused. His frown seemed entirely human, and I was comforted by the readability of his expression. There was a sharp exchange between the person on the screen and one of those who had seized me outside the barn, which was not translated for my benefit. In the end, the man on the screen uttered a single brief syllable, which the machine rendered into English as: 'Impossible.'

"'As you can see perfectly well,' I retorted, stiffly 'it is *not* impossible. I am real; I am a timeshadow; I am here. Will you tell me what kind of man *you* are'

"'I am no man,' replied the other, with apparent contempt, as soon as the machine had translated my words. '*Men* make blood but have no minds. *You* are no man. You have a mind but make no blood. *We* are *overmen*.'

"It was my turn to say: 'What are *overmen*? Explain!'

"It was, I think, the translation machine itself that responded, not the man on the screen. 'Members of the dominant species,' it said. 'End-products of earthly evolution.'

THE HUNGER AND ECSTASY OF VAMPIRES

"'What year is this?' I asked. 'How long has it been since *my* kind were emperors of the earth? How many thousands of years?'

"The man on the screen—or, rather, the *overman* on the screen—shook his head slightly in bewilderment. I took what further comfort I could from the fact that whatever technical miracles were his to command, the science of casting a timeshadow did not seem to be among them. He did not answer my question. Instead, he said: 'You are a strangely solid illusion, if you are indeed an illusion.'

"My first impulse was to take offence, and deny it, but I realised that he was not trying to insult me. He was talking more to himself than to me, giving voice to his incomprehension. 'I came to this world,' I said, 'to see what time would make of *Homo sapiens*, man the wise. I came to see what triumphs and glories lay in store for our descendants. It seems to me that if the earth has passed into the care of *overmen* who use their own kind—their fellow humans—as mere cattle, and milk them of their life-blood, then the news which I must carry back with me is dire and terrible.' I added, as my resolution faltered and I remembered that I had at least as much cause for doubt as he did: 'I must hope, I suppose, that *you* are the strangely solid illusion, and that this is nothing but an opium-dream.'

"While he waited for this speech to be translated, the person on the screen grew much more thoughtful—and so did the others who clustered around me. When he replied, he spoke in a level tone which the translation-machine reproduced.

"'You do not understand,' he said, speaking for the first time as though he were attempting to explain. 'The lovers

of daylight are not our own kind. Humans are not our *fellows*—
in the long-gone days before they became our docile herds,
they were our deadliest enemies. Is that truly what you are: a
wild and savage *human* miraculously preserved since the dawn
of history?' It seemed that the translation machine was having
some slight trouble with the concept of a human being, and I
judged that the implications of the situation were only now
becoming evident to the person on the screen.

"'Some of the human of my own time are wild and
savage,' I told him. 'Some, it is said, still have the cannibal
habit, and will slay their fellow men for food. But I am a *civilized*
man—a man of intelligence and culture.'

"While the translation of my words was being relayed
the door opened again, and the two who had left returned,
the first of them carrying an empty syringe mounted with a
long, glittering needle. I knew at once that he intended to use
it to extract blood from my body—or whatever fluid was
circulating in my shadowy *corpus*.

"I opened my mouth to protest vigorously, and leapt
to my feet in alarm, but the syllables I had tried to pronounce
never sounded, and when I lashed out with my arms they failed
to connect with anything solid. The world had turned to mist,
and was already dissolving into darkness.

"I felt that I was falling into an infinite abyss. I lost
consciousness....and when I awoke again, I was all a-tremble
in my true body, and my good friend the doctor was busy
reassuring himself that I was fit and well, or at least alive and
sensible."

* * * *

9

"I know that some of you will already have formed opinions as to the significance of this strange experience," Copplestone said, looking around at his listeners doubtfully and rather apologetically. "I suppose most of you will be inclined, at least for the moment, to the hypothesis which I offered the overmen in the course of my first encounter with them—that my experience was but a delusion. There is much in it, I know, which is reminiscent of perfectly ordinary dreams. You may well think that vampires are imaginary beings whose mythical origins must be sought in equally ordinary nightmares, and which have no place in rational visions of the future—but I have much more to relate, and I beg you to reserve your final judgment until you have heard accounts of my second and third adventures in time."

He still seemed reasonably strong, and his voice was steady, but his body was slumped in his armchair in a fashion which betrayed considerable fatigue.

As I looked around I could see that I was not the only one anxious on his behalf. I saw, too, that the young man who had spoken to me about the resemblances between Copplestone's tale and his own was very eager to make his complaint generally known, but his curly-haired companion—who had taken a seat beside him—restrained him. He whispered something which I took to be an entreaty to be allowed to speak in the other's stead, and the excitable young man reluctantly gave way to him.

"I think, Dr Copplestone," said the dark-complexioned young man, "that it might be as well to clear up one puzzling point before we hear the continuation of your story. My friend and I have been struck very forcibly by the manner in which your account of the far future duplicates certain features of a series of speculative articles that has been published recently in the *National Observer*. We cannot help but wonder whether your visionary experience might be reproducing—unwittingly, no doubt—a distorted version of these articles, which you might have read or heard discussed."

I watched Copplestone's face very closely. If that were true, I thought, then the distortions of his tale might also have a commonplace source, and the parts of the story which most interested me might also have been borrowed—wittingly or not—from Arminius Vambery, presumably *via* Bram Stoker. The professor, however, seemed genuinely surprised by Mr. Shiel's suggestion.

"I fear that I have read no such articles," he said. "There are so many periodicals in circulation these days that I can hardly keep track of their titles, let alone their contents. My experiments have taken up almost all of my time these last few months, and I have had little contact with anyone save for my servants and my physician. I certainly do not recall discussing anything of this kind, or hearing it discussed—and I am certain that I would have paid very careful attention to any such discussion. There were, I recall, some articles issued a little over a year ago—in the *Pall Mall Budget*, I believe—which the good doctor did bring to my attention. One was entitled 'The Man of the Year Million', another 'The Extinction of Man'. I thought them fascinating, but...."

"They too were mine!" the pale young man interposed, unable to keep silent any longer. "All of this is mine!"

"Yours?" Copplestone's amazement seemed sincere enough to me, but I could not trust my judgment well enough to be absolutely sure. "I am sorry, then, that I did not immediately recognise your name when you were introduced to me. Your presence here is a happy coincidence."

"It is not entirely coincidental, Professor Copplestone," confessed the pale young man's friend. "I suppose that you contacted me because you remembered my interest in certain matters on which your story has touched, expressed *en passant* in the conversations we had before I went to Derbyshire. Having so recently returned, I had no intimate acquaintance I might bring with me, so I, in my turn, wrote to Mr. Wells—whom I hardly know, save by repute—because I knew of his very similar interests. I dare say that there are others here who came with some kind of predisposition to be intrigued. Sir William and Mr. Tesla presumably came to hear your accounts of the electrical machinery of the future. Mr. Wilde and his friend might well be interested in your visionary method—although I have had some experience of opium myself, and I must say that your experience does not seem to me to have the least resemblance to an opium dream."

"I think he has confused you with Stenbock," Wilde whispered to me. "A man born and nursed in the colonies can hardly be expected to be able to tell one Count from another."

I had avoided meeting Stenbock, although I knew that he had asked after me when I first arrived in London. I wanted to avoid encouraging any association between our names that might be ready to take root in the minds of the unwary. No such automatic association could have arisen had the English aristocracy boasted Counts of its own, but the English mind does have a tendency to think of all those who bear foreign titles as a kind of tribe, and I was most certainly not the same kind of madman as Count Stenbock.

"I agree," Copplestone said, in reply to the young man's remark about opium. "Perhaps it was foolish of me to introduce the simile. My time machine is a compound of a very different chemical class, which sharpens very different sensibilities. I wonder if it is possible that Mr. Wells has the kind of natural gift which can perceive the future—albeit dimly—even without such assistance. Except that...."

I saw the white-bearded man of science nod with satisfaction at hearing his own hypothesis repeated, but his companion scowled, and I judged that in Mr. Tesla's view one improbability was now being piled atop another. Given that there was a much more ordinary way by which Mr. Wells's ideas could have influenced Dr Copplestone, I was half-inclined to agree with him. And yet, Copplestone's story did seem sincere.

Copplestone, after pausing briefly to reflect, began again. "May I ask, sir," he said to the excitable young man, "whether your story continues beyond a point parallel to that which my own has reached?"

"In the *National Observer* version, no," Wells replied. "but I have now completed a revised version which is somewhat longer. But even if the continuation of your story reproduces that part of the story, the similarity might still be accountable without our being close kin to Nostradamus. Henley has seen it, and half a dozen others. There are a dozen ways the rumour could have got around."

"That is a pity," said Copplestone. "It would have been more interesting had there been no possible way for me to have knowledge of that of which, I assure you, I have in fact no knowledge at all. I wonder, however, whether our stories continue to run along parallel paths, or whether they diverge. May I ask whether your story deals, after the fashion of your earlier essays, with the man of the year million and the extinction of man?"

"The former, no," said the young man, a little suspiciously. "The latter, yes. The extinction of man *on earth* is, of course, inevitable and must be the end-point of any future history. As the sun gradually fades to a mere ember, as it must while it exhausts the fuel of its combustion, the surface of the earth will become uninhabitable by life as we know it—and that is how my story concludes. Men may find habitats elsewhere, of course, but on earth their day will be done in a million years, or a few millions at most."

"That is most interesting," said Copplestone, judiciously. "The span of time involved in my adventures does not, I fear, extend to millions of years. It does include, in a manner of speaking, the extinction of man, but the earth does not become uninhabitable and man's successors— who are not quite what I deduced as a result of my first expedition into the future—continue to thrive. I think that if you will agree to be patient for a while, you might well find that any resemblance between your story and mine will disappear by degrees."

THE HUNGER AND ECSTASY OF VAMPIRES

The young man was not unduly impressed by this. I could see, however, that several other members of the company had by now become impatient with this question of borrowing, and desired it to be laid aside so that we might proceed. It was Wilde who appointed himself the spokesman for this group.

"If I may say so," he said, mildly, "this digression is unhelpful. There will be time enough to discuss the possible provenance of your story when we have heard it all, and I am perfectly happy—as Mr. Wells must surely be—to accept your word that no deliberate borrowing of ideas has taken place."

Mr. Wells shrugged his shoulders. "I suppose I should accept the similarity as an endorsement of my own powers of foresight," he muttered, sarcastically. He seemed to take little comfort in the notion that other prophets might come forward—an entire legion of them, if Copplestone's formula were ever to be published—to testify to the accuracy of his story. I could understand that he might feel an awkward conflict between his desire to be reckoned an accurate prophet and his desire to be reckoned an original artist.

"There is no way to prove the truthfulness of this story," said Tesla, seemingly keen to distance himself from Sir William's suggestion that both Copplestone and Wells might be tapping the same occult power of precognition. "If it *is* the record of a dream concocted by Copplestone's mind, the continuance of similar themes in subsequent dreams would be perfectly understandable—even in dreams experienced by others who had heard the story before taking the drug. If you really desire someone else to check your revelations they must take your drug *without* any advance warning of what they might expect to see under its influence."

THE HUNGER AND ECSTASY OF VAMPIRES

"On the other hand," the older man of science put in, whimsically, "any one of us who accepts Copplestone's invitation to sample his elixir could not conclude that his vision is inaccurate if they go into the experiment armed with a conviction that he is a liar."

"I can assure you," Tesla said, "that I have not the slightest intention of offering myself as a guinea-pig for...."

"Gentlemen!" Wilde protested. "We are wasting time. If we do not hear the resumption of Professor Copplestone's story soon, we shall be here till dawn."

"I hope we shall not be delayed so long as that," I murmured, supportively. "It would be most inconvenient."

"You are quite right," said Copplestone, hastily. "I am glad that Mr. Wells has brought the matter of the similarity between my story and his to our attention, and I admit the relevance of what Sir William and Mr. Tesla have said, but I do think that we should press on. If there is no objection, I will begin immediately to offer an account of the further exploits of my timeshadow."

There was no objection. I was evidently not the only one who did not relish the thought that the business might take all night.

* * * *

10

"For the purposes of my second excursion in far futurity I increased the dosage of the drug by a third," Copplestone said. "The good and dutiful doctor expressed strong reservations about the wisdom of this course, but the after-effects of my first expedition seemed to have been been relatively mild, and in my enthusiasm for discovery I thought the risk justified.

"I had no way of knowing exactly how far into the future my first expedition had taken me, and I had no way of knowing how much further the increased dose would impel me, but I believed that I would be able to span several times as many years. Although no firm evidence had been presented to me in the course of my first expedition I judged that it must have taken me at least several thousand years into the future. I now hoped to see what might have become of the earth after several tens of thousands.

"The sensation of displacement followed the familiar pattern, and I found myself once again standing on a hillside lit by a warm summer sun that had passed its zenith. I was reassured by the fact that it was daylight, but I knew that I would have to face nightfall eventually, and that if the world were still ruled by the vampire race I had encountered in my first expedition then I was almost certain to encounter them again.

"I was dressed exactly as I had been before. My timeshadow seemed even heavier, and when I touched my breast it seemed perfectly solid. The slope on which I found myself was densely wooded, and there was no way to tell whether or not it was the same spot on the earth's surface to which I had come previously.

"I was surrounded by the sound of birdsong and the faint hum of insect wings, and I must admit that I experienced a sharp pang of disappointment because I could see nothing in my immediate vicinity to assure me that this was not my own time. Although I could not name the various species to which the surrounding trees belonged my knowledge of botany was inadequate to make me certain that they were alien to my experience, and in their general features they were very similar to those one might find in any of the woodlands of the shires.

"I began to walk in the direction which I had taken previously, heading for the place where I had joined the roadway which had taken me into the town where the human cattle lived. Although my timeshadow was more cumbersome I now had some ready-made understanding of how to adapt myself, and it was not long began to feel reasonably competent and fairly comfortable. While I cultivated a normal gait I practised pronouncing familiar syllables, schooling my deep and awkward voice until I could produce what sounded to my own ears like an acceptable version of the English language. I did not suppose for an instant that anyone I met might be able to understand any words I spoke, but I wanted to avoid the embarrassment of seeming stupidly inarticulate to anyone I did happen to meet.

The Hunger and Ecstasy of Vampires

"After ten or twelve minutes of walking I became aware of the fact that a particular insect, about the size of a house-fly or honey-bee, was always close to my head. I tried to shoo it away, but it easily evaded my flapping hand, and circled around just beyond my reach, stubbornly refusing to depart. When I walked faster, the insect accelerated; although it made no attempt to settle upon my person it insisted on keeping close attendance with me. I could not see it with perfect clarity because it was perpetually on the move, but its species was unknown to me; it certainly was not a house-fly or a bee, although it had a dark, rounded body and a small head bearing what seemed to be two complex antennae. In the end, I decided to ignore the creature.

"When I reached the floor of the valley, where the road might or might not have been in much earlier times, I found a sluggish and murky stream. It was not very deep, but it was wide enough not to be jumped with perfect safety, and in any case there seemed to be no particular reason why I should want to get to the other side. I turned to my left, following the direction of the stream's flow.

"I followed the course of the meandering stream for several hundred yards. I had fallen silent by now, and I was moving fluently enough to make very little noise. Eventually, I came to the rim of a little waterfall, where the stream tumbled down into a pool some five or six feet below. The rim of the little cliff was bordered by bushes, but I was tall enough to see over them—and in the hollow below, I saw a strange figure kneeling to drink from the stream. I stopped instantly, frozen by shock. I had been fully prepared to find the world utterly changed, and had thought that there was nothing I might find in such a far future which could astonish me, but I had not expected *this*.

"It was a satyr: a creature with the torso and belly of a man and hindquarters which would have been more fitting on a goat.

"The creature's head was very hairy, and two small horns projected from his forehead. The only thing which did not quite match the classical image of a satyr was his feet, which were far more massive than a goat's, though they seemed as horny as hooves and certainly bore no toes. He was slight of stature and slender in the body, no more massive than a healthy thirteen-year-old boy, but his face, strangely compounded out of human and animal features, somehow gave the impression of extreme age.

"*How can this possibly be the future?* I asked myself. *It could not even be the past, into which I might have slipped had my timeshadow been displaced in the wrong direction, for satyrs never really existed. They are figments of the human imagination: creatures born of superstitious fantasy. One species of fabulous creature might be explicable, but to encounter fauns as well a vampires is surely proof positive that all this is a mere dream, that there is nothing in it but the produce of mere fancy.*

"My disappointment was, however, alleviated by curiosity. *Well then*, I thought, *If I am removed to Hesiod's Age of Gold or Silver, I must make the most of it. If satyrs have replaced vampires as the dominant species of my delusion, then I must be careful to study satyrs more closely and more competently than I was able to study vampires.*

"I must have been staring at the creature for about ten seconds before he suddenly became aware of my presence—I cannot say how—and turned to look up at me. I could not easily read his expression, so I could not tell how astonished he might be by the sight of me, but at least he did not start with alarm and flee in panic.

"He stood up slowly, and turned slightly so as to face me squarely. Then he proceeded to stare at me as steadily as I was staring at him. After ten or twelve seconds he threw back his head and uttered a loud sound, which seemed far less human than his head or legs. It was a sound which human vocal chords could not have made, more closely resembling the note of some huge musical instrument like a church organ. Like a phrase from some atonal composition it rose and fell, echoing eerily from the bank on which I stood.

"Afterwards, there was silence. For a few moments I did not know whether he had sounded a warning or an expression of feeling—but I quickly realised that it must have been a summons, or at least an invitation. From the trees around the clearing other figures appeared.

"In Greek myth, if I remember rightly, fauns and satyrs were exclusively male, and their chief delight was the pursuit of delicately human-seeming nymphs. Here, by contrast, there were females of the species too, and children. The females were less shaggy in the shanks, and the hair on their heads was less coarse, but no one seeing them in daylight could possibly have mistaken them for humans, Their features were a similar compound of human and animal, and their feet were every bit as strange.

"Within the space of a few minutes a company of thirteen had gathered, five of which were little ones—one of them a babe in arms. They did not menace me in any way. Like the one who had summoned them, they simply stared, with what I took to be frank curiosity. They did not beckon to me, but I received the impression that they were waiting for me to join them.

"I found a place where I could scramble down the bank, and did so, though very awkwardly. At the bottom, which I reached rather too hurriedly, I sprawled in a most ungainly fashion. I was not winded, but I could not immediately rise, and one of the fauns approached me tentatively, his hand outstretched. I took it, and he helped me up. I was more than a foot taller than he, but he seemed very strong.

"'Thank you,' I said, letting go of his slender, warm fingers. The sound of my voice, so different from his own, did not alarm him. He continued to stare up into my eyes, so intently that I wished I could read his unhuman expression.

"'Are you mere animals in human form?' I said, speaking in what I hoped was a reassuring tone. 'Or are you intelligent beings whose mode of thought is too alien to permit sensible communication?'

"The bushes parted again, and another creature came out. This one was of another kind, and for one brief moment I though he might be a man. He was very much taller than the dwarfish fauns, and far more manlike in the face, but as his hindquarters emerged from the undergrowth which at first concealed them I saw that he too was only half-human.

"He was a centaur of sorts, although his lower body did not much resemble that of a horse; it was more like that of a sleek brown bear. Like all the rest he stood still and stared at me from a distance, reaching up with an oddly delicate hand to stroke his lank brown beard. Then he spoke, or seemed to speak, to the satyr who had sounded the summons. His voice was not in the least manlike, nor did it resemble the whinnying of a horse; again, it was like a series of profound notes sounded by a musical instrument.

"The faun replied. I could not tell for sure whether their speech was meaningful; it might or might not have been language.

"Again the thought occurred to me that perhaps I had made a mistake and cast my timeshadow into the distant past before the race of men came into being, and that my mind had seen fit to populate its emptiness according to the imagination of the first story-tellers. It took only a moment or two, however, for me to understand that I might have it all the wrong way around. I realised that the images of the past which ancient societies possessed might well have been based on misinterpretations of the glimpses of the distant future which their seers had caught.

"I already knew, of course, that the priest-magicians of ancient societies had used much the same drugs which gave their modern equivalents access to premonitory visions. The most gifted among them, I knew, must always have had the power to journey into the farther reaches of time, but they had never been able to *stabilise* their timeshadows as I had contrived to do. Even I was unable as yet properly to calibrate the impulse of my time machine, and did not know exactly when in time I might be; it was, therefore, entirely understandable that those ancient visionaries had located the Golden Age in the past rather than the future, and made it part of their fantasies of Creation and Descent.

"This conclusion raised my spirits considerably. I became convinced that I *was* in the future, and that it was an *actual* future—at the very least a future of contingency, and perhaps the one and only future of destiny. But was there more to this future, I wondered, than gentle and uncommunicative chimeras? Had I any chance of finding out what had happened during the vast gulf of time which separated this seemingly-happy era from the age in which vampires had ruled the world?

"Impulsively, I stepped towards the centaur, and reached out my hand as though to clasp his. He did not shy away, but nor did he reach out in friendship. His face showed no detectable expression.

"*He is an animal, I thought, despite his human features—but he does not fear me! Either he is perfectly tame or he thinks me one of his own kind, a freakish cousin.*

"I stepped back so that I could look at all the assembled crowd. I raised my arms, palms open, in a gesture which was intended to signal farewell and reassurance.

"'I must go on,' I said to them, apologetically. 'I have not much time, and I must see as much of your world as I can, even if I cannot reach the edge of the forest before the elastic thread which attaches me to my own time snatches me back again.'

"I felt a slight thrill of triumph as they copied me, one and all. With the sole exception of the tiny child, they raised their arms, exactly as I had done—and their imitation suggested to me a kind of kinship which ran far deeper than any partial similarity of form.

"At that moment, however, I was reminded once again of the insect which had kept close company with me since the moments immediately following my arrival. It descended to fly around my head, buzzing more loudly than before—and it was no longer alone.

"Within a few seconds there were a dozen of the tiny flying things, and within a few seconds more there were hundreds. I flapped my arms at them reflexively, as fearful as though I were being attacked by a whole swarm of stinging bees, and although I half-closed my eyes against the imagined assault I saw that the satyrs and the centaur had similarly began to swat the air. This time their gestures were not mere imitation; the hollow seemed to be filling up with a coalescing cloud, and the air itself seemed to be abuzz with a vast, all-pervading sound.

"The centaur and his companions turned to run away, possessed now by the panic which the sight of me had failed to induce. They ran away from the stream, into the depths of the wood, but I ran a different way, continuing along the course I had set, parallel to the slow watercourse.

"I, and I alone, was pursued by the swarm. It was as difficult to run in this world as it had been in the earlier one, and I was once again painfully aware of the difficulty. I must have known almost immediately that I could not possibly outrun the tiny things which buzzed around my head if they were disposed to follow me, but my fear was unreasoning. I have always been afraid of bees and wasps, and the behaviour of the insects now seemed to me to be exactly that of a swarm of angry bees, so I ran in terror.

"I must have blundered on, ineffectually, for several hundred yards. My frightened mind could not quite grasp the fact that I had not been stung, and that not one of the insects had actually settled upon me. But I could not run for long; I was too clumsy. I caught my foot upon a trailing root and stumbled. I managed to stop myself sprawling full length, but I fell to my knees, flailing my arms. It seemed that my flailing was not without effect, for there were not so many of the insects about my head now. They were moving ahead of me, as though to anticipate the resumption of my headlong flight, and I cursed their apparent determination to block my way.

"While I remained where I was, trying hard to catch my breath, I saw that the whole vast swarm was now coming together. The vague cloud, assembling itself some ten or twelve feet away from me, began to take on a definite shape, which became ever more distinct.

"As I lowered my arms, because there seemed no further need to defend myself, I saw that the shape which the cloud of insects was assuming was approximately human. While I watched, far more astonished now than I had been before, it seemed that they ceased to be insects at all, and became the cells of an upright body: a human figure which looked like an animate bronze statue, its surface as smooth as silk.

"The terror which I felt did not in the least abate as I watched his miracle. I could not conceive that any being supernaturally distilled from a horde of noxious insects could be anything but loathsome and malevolent. Whereas the fauns and the centaur had never seemed anything but harmless in their docile innocence, this monstrous homunculus struck me as a veritable demon.

"In the course of my unusually eventful life I have been in many hazardous situations, and have often survived by virtue of keeping my head when others might have lost theirs—but on this occasion, I confess, I lost my head completely. When I managed to get to my feet, convinced that the monster intended to impede my further progress, I hurled myself at it, striking out violently with my fists, as though to batter it to the ground. I was a fool, of course. My timeshadow-arms were woefully weak *and the object of my attack was less than solid.* My blows

THE HUNGER AND ECSTASY OF VAMPIRES

passed clean through it, not because it was as insubstantial as a ghost, but because its myriad components simply gave way and flew momentarily apart as I stuck at it, presenting no resistance.

"I fell again, more heavily this time. I felt bruised and sore, and wondered once more how direly the damage I suffered as a timeshadow might be communicated back to my body when—or if—I became whole again.

"The swarm coalesced once again into that hideous golem, which now seemed to be a mocking reflection of my own form. It had my height and my girth, and it did not seem to me that this was mere coincidence.

"Then, in a seeming travesty of the gesture which the faun had made when I slipped down the bank into the hollow, it stretched out a 'hand', offering to help me up. I could not bring myself to take it; I simply stared at the horrible thing, paralysed by fear. It seemed as solid as a statue now; there was no indication of the fact that it was compounded out of thousands of ubiquitous units.

"It slowly lowered the proffered arm. Then it opened its brazen mouth and spoke.

"The syllables were as deep and as hoarse and as hollow as the words which had spilled from my own mouth while I practised the art of pronunciation, but they were quite distinct and there was no mistaking the word they pronounced—the *name* they pronounced.

"'Cop-ple-stone!' said the monster, laboriously. 'Cop-ple-stone!'"

* * * *

11

Copplestone paused, as if for dramatic effect. He still seemed distinctly ill, but there was an excitement in his manner that was no mere physical fever. He knew that none of us could any longer complain that his tale was too dull or that its imagery lacked flair. We waited patiently for him to continue.

"Had my anxiety been capable of increase," he went on, "the fact that the monster could pronounce my name might have sent yet another thrill of terror coursing through my attenuated form, but I felt that nothing further could be added to my distress. I seized upon the golem's use of my name as a puzzle to be solved.

"While I asked myself feverishly how such a miracle could be the creature compounded out of the swarm of false insects stood stock still, waiting for me to rise. As time passed, moment by moment, without my being rent or crushed by those metallic hands, the puzzle was able to take command of my thoughts and drive the panic out.

"My sense of physical danger was still acute. I knew, however, that there was little to be gained by trying to run away from the golem, and that it would be a better use of my time and effort to discover its purpose.

"'How do you know my name?' I demanded, breathlessly, amazed by my own temerity. 'Can you read my thoughts?'

"The mechanical golem waved its arm in what seemed to be a negative gesture.

"'Copplestone,' it said, speaking with a little more assurance now that it had heard my reply. 'Are you Copplestone?'

"'That is my name,' I said. 'I ask again—how do you know it?' The golem took a step towards me, but I did not flinch. It was not so much the words it had spoken that had calmed me, but that I had spoken to it, tacitly accepting it as a thinking being. It reached out its hand again, and this time I took it.

"It felt as hard as polished metal, but it was not cold. It did no more than support me while I pulled myself up, but I had the impression that it was very strong. The tiny things which had combined to make it had knitted together perfectly to make a single seamless body.

"'Thank you,' I said. 'What are you?'

"It did not reply to my question. I stood face to face with it now, and I looked into its eyes. It did have eyes of a sort—black orbs, of a subtly different texture from the surrounding bronze—but they were infinitely more alien than the eyes of the faun or the eyes of the centaur. Its face now seemed less hideous to me than it had been; indeed, its features seemed very ordinary, though not particularly handsome. Its cheeks were contoured like a man's, although I could not believe that there were similar muscles beneath the outer tegument, and it had a nose of sorts, but devoid of nostrils. Its mouth was a black slit, whose border was shaped to give a sketchy impression of lips. Its metallic complexion was nearer to the colour of mahogany than to bronze.

"When we had stared at one another for a few seconds it hesitantly extended its hand again, plainly unsure as to whether I would condescend to take it or not. I remembered that the centaur had not been able to respond to my similar gesture. I took it, exactly as though I were shaking hands with a new acquaintance. Its grasp was gentle enough, not at all like a grip of steel.

"'Copplestone,' it said, yet again. Its powers of communication were evidently rather limited. 'You are Copplestone.'

"The fact that it could pronounce those syllables was a miracle beyond compare—provided, of course, that I really was in a future thousands of years further from my own time than the one I had visited before. Yet again, I began to doubt that. A man may always be recognised in his dreams; whatever phantoms are conjured up in his imagination may have access to his most intimate secrets.

"'How do you know me?' I asked, again. My fear had by now transmuted itself into a keen sense of absurdity—and this too seemed reminiscent of the emotional confusion which afflicts a dreaming man. Could something as strange and bizarre as this automaton made of insects, I wondered, be a product of my own fevered imagination? Could it possibly be anything else? And what of the fauns and the centaur? How could they possibly belong to a true future?

"The golem opened its arms wide, as if to embrace me. 'Come,' it said. 'Be not afraid!'

I stood where I was.

"'Be not afraid!' it repeated. There was little or no

inflection in its mechanical voice. It could not contrive to sound reassuring, nor could it plead.

"'Where?' I asked. It was the wrong question. The golem did not want me to go with it; it merely wanted me to step into its embrace. When I would not do so, it stepped forward to take me. As it did so, its countless units came apart again, but it did not break up into a flying swarm; instead, it *flowed* around and over me, enclosing me.

"It formed a new body, around my own, fitting itself about me like a suit of living armour.

"I understood why it had instructed me not to be afraid, but the instruction was impossible to obey. I was all too well aware of the fact that it could crush the life out of me by a slight adjustment of its shape.

"I tried to protest, but no words came forth—but it had the courtesy, or the common sense, to leave my face uncovered. I could breathe and I could see.

"*If this is a dream, I told myself, sternly, you will surely wake up before anything too terrible can happen. If it is not, and this really is the future, you will come to no harm. Your name is known, and your coming must have been awaited for thousands of years. You are precious here, infinitely precious....*

"I began to move. It was not, of course, by my own volition, but according to the will of the entity which enclosed me. It began to run, swiftly accelerating its pace to a sprint. Had I tried to achieve such a velocity using the ghostly muscles of my timeshadow it would have required enormous effort, but because the motive force was provided by my captor I felt for the first time that I really was a kind of phantom, lighter than the air.

"I could have spoken aloud. I could have asked 'Where are we going?'—but how would the golem have responded, now that it no longer had a mouth?

"Thus cocooned, I was taken through the forest for many a mile—or so at least it seemed. But we came before very long to a clearing where stood a huge iron mast, more than a hundred feet high, and a number of low huts, and several strange machines with rounded bodies and long tails, each with four long horizontal vanes on top and four much smaller ones arranged vertically at the extremity of the tail.

"I expected to be taken to one of the huts, but I was taken instead to one of these machines. My suit of armour opened a hatch in the belly of one of them, and climbed in. It was very dark inside—there were no windows, and little light crept in from below—so I could only judge what happened next by means of touch. This was very difficult at first, for I remained enclosed inside my mechanical shell, insulated from direct contact, but after some wriggling I ended up in a sitting position, and I felt my armour flow away again, to leave me largely uncovered, but not free. I was still secured by bands about my arms, legs and waist, so that my movements were severely restricted.

"My ears were filled with a sound like the droning of a million insects, and I wondered if the swarm of golem-parts was breaking up again, but it came from all around and it did not abate. A sinking sensation in my stomach told me that the machine in whose belly I was now enclosed was lifting from the ground, and I knew that I had simply been transferred from one prison to another: from a running-machine to a flying-machine. My journey was not ended; it had hardly begun.

THE HUNGER AND ECSTASY OF VAMPIRES

"The hatchway through which I had entered the machine was closed now, and I was in pitch darkness for two or three minutes, but then light returned. It was not diffuse light, like the artificial phosphorescence which had lit the town and the Underworld of my previous vision; it was highly localized within a space in front of my head. It was almost as though I were looking into an illuminated aquarium, for the illuminated space had a curious *liquid* quality about it—but there were no fish swimming there.

"Instead, there was a disembodied head.

"Although disembodied, the head was far from dead, and seemed quite undiscomfited by its detachment. Its features were animated and not unhandsome, but I knew immediately that it was not a man. I recognized the pallid complexion, the blackish lips and the cat-like eyes. It was an overman—or, at least, the *image* of an overman. I knew that there was nothing really *there*, and that even the impression of three-dimensionality must be an illusion. Either this was someone speaking to me from afar, his image relayed by some mechanical process of reproduction which ignored his body, or it was a synthesized image, a mere simulacrum of life.

"'Are you truly Copplestone?' the face said. At any rate, those were the words which came from a speaker somewhere above the image; the dark lips moved to pronounce quite different syllables, and I inferred that some kind of translation machine was again being used.

"'I am,' I replied, hoarsely.

"'From what time do you come, Copplestone?' he asked.

"'From the nineteenth century *Anno Domini*,' I told him.

THE HUNGER AND ECSTASY OF VAMPIRES

"The expression on his face shifted, and he seemed perplexed. There followed a long hesitation. I leapt to the conclusion that he had no idea what *Anno Domini* meant, but did not know how to ask for clarification. I realised that if he somehow had access to the substance of the conversation which I had had with his remote ancestor, so many thousands of years before, he might know a little about me, but not very much .

"'I am Edward Copplestone,' I told him, proudly. 'I am the pioneer of the exploration of the future. Others will doubtless follow where I have led, but none can come from any earlier time for more than the fleetest moment, nor bring more than a faint echo of substance with them. Is that why you set your insectile machines to keep watch for my timeshadow? Is that why I am a miracle in your eyes?'

"The face reacted to my words, but the essence of the reaction still seemed to be perplexity and puzzlement. I realised that although I could hardly claim to have the upper hand in the exchange, my interlocutor was struggling under a burden of ignorance and incomprehension as great as my own.

"*He does not understand,* I repeated to myself, trying to reason through the difficulty. *Although he knows my name, he does not know who or what I am. For whatever reason, my example has not been followed by countless others. Visitation by timeshadow is not a commonplace of this future. It must be the case that these so-called overmen, unlike the mere men they have displaced, have no innate capacity for precognition?*

"'Tell me the exact day and hour from which you came,' said the disembodied head, in a fashion which may not have been intended to sound peremptory, but did.

"I was suddenly struck by a fit of suspicion, and hesitated before replying. 'Why should you want to know that?' I asked. 'You can only have the vaguest notion of what the phrase Anno Domini means, so what use would exactitude be?'

"He frowned—and no matter how vast the expanse of time was that separated us, or what differences there might be between his species and mine, it was an unmistakable gesture of annoyance. 'Answer,' he said.

"I resented the implication of command.

"*Perhaps my secret was lost,* I thought. *But if so, how? What prevented me from making it known, from giving all mankind the power of clear foresight. Is it possible—is it even imaginable—that this bodiless thing desires to know my point of origin in order to take action against me, to prevent my revealing what I know about the fate which awaits mankind? Can these overmen be so worldly wise that they can now reach backwards through time to annul events which threaten their reality?*

"These thoughts were, of course, very confused. There was far too much to think about, and the head still wanted its answer. I decided that I must be cautious, at least until I knew more.

"'I have many questions of my own,' I retorted. 'And I have not much time to ask them. You must know a great deal already about my world, while I know nothing at all about yours, save that your kind once reduced mine to the level of mere cattle, which you milked for blood. Why are you so curious about me, when all the curiosity should be on my side?'

"He looked at me very carefully, as though he could not make up his mind what to say. He seemed remarkably unintelligent, considering all the marvellous machines which he had at his disposal. Was he, I wondered, no more than a machine himself—another golem, able to reproduce the semblance of a person, but only capable of limited intellectual performance?

"'Be not afraid,' he said. 'I desire to learn.'

"'I repeat that there is much more for me to learn about you than you could possibly learn from me,' I said. 'I do not even know what manner of man—or *overman*—you are. If appearances can be trusted, your forefathers bred mine for their blood, and hence were vampires of a kind. Given that, how should I begin to trust you, and why should I tell you anything at all?'

"He frowned again, but I could not read any wrath in his frown.

"'Answer,' he said, impotently. 'Be not afraid.'

"I knew him then for some kind of parrot, trained to talk but not to make proper sense. 'I am not afraid,' I lied, 'but I am not a fool. I refuse to talk to golems and disembodied heads, if they cannot tell me what I ardently desire to know. I am your prisoner, forced to go wherever you care to take me, but I have nothing to say to you unless you will condescend to contribute to my enlightenment. *You* must answer *me*!"

The image flickered, as though the 'fluid' in the 'aquarium' had been rippled by the current of my displeasure. The features of the face shifted eerily, but then were reconstituted.

"'Ask," said the head, emotionlessly. 'Ask, and I will answer.'

"I felt a surge of triumph, but restrained my exultation.

THE HUNGER AND ECSTASY OF VAMPIRES

"'Is yours truly a race of vampires?' I asked. 'Did your kind enslave mine, at some point in our mutual history, and reduce the descendants of man to mere animality? Is mankind now extinct?'

"'In a time of trial, thousands of years ago,' the head reported, 'your descendants fought with my ancestors, and were subdued. Once subdued, they were bred for blood and not for brains, and in the space of a few hundred generations became as docile and as unintelligent as cattle or swine. Overmen no longer need the blood of human beings, but there was no way to return to humankind what humankind had lost: sentience, intelligence, free will. My more recent forefathers chose a different way: they remade human beings in the myriad images of ancient human dreams, and gave them a garden in which to live contentedly. One day, that garden will span a continent—perhaps, in the very distant future, it might cover all the earth—but the human race can never recover its intelligence unless that garden becomes a wilderness of a very much harsher kind. The descendants of humankind will only make progress if they first rediscover the constant threat of pain and death.'

"This recitation was delivered as though it were a dull lecture of no particular substance. There was no trace of emotion in it, nor of apology.

"I am, of course, thoroughly familiar with Charles Darwin's theory of evolution by natural selection, and I had no difficulty in following the argument which had been so starkly laid out for me. For the same reason, though, I was sorely puzzled as to the origins of the race which called now themselves *overmen*.

"'If your forefathers were not mine,' I said to him, 'where did they come from? Were they invaders from the planet Mars?'

THE HUNGER AND ECSTASY OF VAMPIRES

"'Your kind and mine had common ancestors,' he said. He did not elaborate, and I felt slightly frustrated, wondering whether the inadequacy of the answer was deliberate dissimulation.

"'Are you, then, the children of the vampires of legend?' I said, wondering if his translation-machinery was capable of detecting sarcasm. 'Were your distant ancestors the reanimated corpses of wicked men, returned from the grave to feed upon their brethren?'

"'No,' he said, flatly. "'Not that. When do you come from, Copplestone? What moment? What place? Your language is English—did you come from England?'

"I knew that I ought to honour my bargain, but still I could not help but wonder why he wanted the information, and whether I might endanger myself by giving it. 'English was the language of the greater part of the globe,' I told him, feeling free to exaggerate the truth. 'It was spoken throughout an empire on which the sun never set. It was the language of Australasia and North America as well as the British Isles.'

"'But it was England from which you came?' he persisted.

"'Where are we going?' I countered. The question was prompted because the flying machine had begun to descend again, and I was aware of a progressive deceleration. 'Where have you brought me?'

"'You are here,' he answered, sourly. I wondered how much comfort he took in the triviality of the answer.

"I felt the bonds which had restrained me flowing away. By the time that the belly of the machine began to open beneath my feet I was free, and a ramp extended itself so that I might let myself down to the ground. The disembodied head disappeared, and when I reached out my hand I found that there was nothing there but a blank wall.

"*Illusion*, I said to myself. *Thus far, all has been illusion. Thus far!*

"Then I stepped down from the flying-machine, ready to meet the true masters of this alien future in the flesh."

* * * *

12

Copplestone stopped speaking again. Whatever medicine had been used to revive him, its effect had suddenly worn off. He was now more haggard and drawn than before, and all the excitement that had possessed him had drained out of him.

The doctor had risen, and was at his side. "It's too much, Ned," he said, softly. "You cannot go on—not tonight, at any rate."

"I must," said Copplestone. "Don't you see that. *I must!*"

The professor was clearly distressed. My companions moved uncomfortably in their chairs, and I knew that some of them must have been convinced by now that Copplestone was deranged. I, on the other hand, had begun to think differently. My anxiety had vanished, and keen curiosity had taken its place.

What if it were true? I thought. *What if he is right, and there is truth in this—truth, perhaps, polluted by fear and fancy, but truth nevertheless?*

I, at least, did not want the professor to stop now. I wanted to hear more, if he were able to offer us more. I wanted to hear the story's conclusion, whether it required all night to reach it or not.

THE HUNGER AND ECSTASY OF VAMPIRES

"Tomorrow is another day," said the doctor, firmly.

Copplestone laughed bitterly, but the laugh immediately dissolved into a fit of coughing. "I know *that*," he whispered, when he could speak again. "Pour me a brandy, my dear fellow."

The doctor was on the brink of refusing the request, but something about Copplestone's eyes would not let him do it. He went to the side-table where the servant had set a decanter and eight crystal glasses, and he poured out a stiff measure. "Anyone else?" he said, as he took it back to Copplestone. Wilde got up to take a glass himself, but no one else went with him.

"I must go on," said Copplestone, to all of us. "There is so much to *explain*. You must forgive me if I sometimes say too much, and sometimes too little, but *I must explain*. I will try to be brief, in the interests of saving my strength."

I could not help but wonder whether he really feared that the inhabitants of the far future might be able to reach back through time and snuff out his life like a candle-flame. Why would they want to, even if they could? Did he think that this was the one and only chance he would have to communicate the secrets he had learned? Could he possibly be arrogant enough to suppose that the entire future of the human race might depend on what he said to us tonight—that destiny itself might be set aside if he could only empower us to act, and save the human race from the fate which awaited it?

Suppose it were so, I told myself. *Is it not a wonderful conceit? It ought to be true. It ought to be the case that the world itself is hanging in the balance, weighed by this strange company, composed of men of letters and men of science....and me.*

THE HUNGER AND ECSTASY OF VAMPIRES

Whatever the reason for his urgency might be, Copplestone was very determined not to bring his discourse to a close while he still had the strength to speak.

"The sun had set," he continued, in a voice hardly above a whisper, "and twilight had all but faded from the sky. Even so, the vista which lay before my eyes was visible, and utterly breathtaking. The perch to which the bird-machine had brought me was high on the side of a mountain, and I only had to move three paces away to look out over a huge plain, which was covered from horizon to horizon by a vast city. All of its streets and most of its buildings were richly illuminated, and the tallest buildings loomed up above the streets with an awesome grandeur.

"In the largest buildings light shone within hundreds, if not thousands, of windows. This was brighter light by far than the diffuse illumination which had leavened the gloom of the barn where the overmen of old bled their human cattle, but it had the same curious blue-violet tint, which my eyes still found uncomfortable.

"I could see tiny flying-machines moving between the buildings, some lit from within by the same eerie light. Many were like the one which had delivered me here but others were differently-designed. I moved closer to the edge of the cliff in order to study the city more closely. There was a guard-rail there, and I rested my hands gingerly upon it. From this coign of vantage it was easy to see that the streets were laid out with remarkable precision, in a vast rectangular grid. Traffic flowed along each and every street in an endless stream, but it was difficult to see any details of the vehicles even though each one lit its own way with twin violet beams. At each intersection the passage of the vehicles was restricted by changing lights which shifted from turquoise to vivid blue to pale violet and back again, in endless succession.

"'Copplestone?' said a voice behind me, and I turned.

"There were two of them; one male and one female. Their faces resembled the disembodied head which had questioned me during the flight, but these were real individuals of flesh and blood. They had no lantern with them, but the light shining from the windows of the solitary house from which they had come allowed me to see them reasonably clearly. They were dressed entirely in black, the male in a suit which displayed his contours as closely as my white 'clothing' displayed mine, the female in a narrow ankle-length skirt. That touch of quasi-human femininity struck me as a remarkable oddity, and I had to wonder yet again whether it was not the sort of detail which betrayed the influence of my own imagination—evidence that this was, at least in part, a dream rather than a true vision of the future.

"The male spoke again, in a voice redolent with wonderment: 'Are you *truly* Copplestone?' He was speaking English, and the words came from his own lips without the aid of any translation-machine, but he pronounced the words as if he were uncertain whether they could possibly mean anything. To him, you see, I was as much a creature of myth as the satyrs and the centaur had been to me. In a world which was to him a long-lost antiquity I had appeared, and disappeared, and there had been no way of knowing whether I would ever return—and yet, there had been hope enough that I might warrant keeping some kind of watch, even for millennia. And there were overmen with leisure enough—and interest enough—to have learned to speak a long-dead language, in order to immerse themselves more fully in the study of a long-dead culture. The machines—the golem and the flying-machine—might have brought me to the one place on earth where there were overmen who could speak to me, who could answer the questions which I so desperately wanted to ask.

"The female came closer, and reached out a delicate hand to touch my forehead. I permitted it. Her fingertips felt slightly damp as she rested them on my brow for half a minute. She said nothing, as if she simply wanted to make sure that I was real, with substance enough to be touched.

"I felt quite calm, now. All my fear had ebbed away, and I was perfectly composed. Later, I wondered whether I might perhaps have been mesmerized, but at the time I simply accepted my condition as natural, and I cannot say that I saw anything at all in her catlike eyes to make me suspect that her gaze might be making a captive of my soul.

"It was the man who led me inside the house, when his consort stepped back again. I did not study the house very closely, but I know that its walls were all curved, without a single corner to be seen, and that its tiled roofs were like conical turrets.

"They took me into a room lit by violet light, but caused the light to be muted so that it would not hurt my eyes. There were no screens on the walls here, and no control-panels—only furniture of a fairly commonplace kind, and a strange device like a fountain enclosed in a globe of glass, where some dark fluid circulated in an agitated manner. Because of the peculiar lighting I could not judge its true colour, but they did not intend to mislead me. They took me to stand before it, and told me frankly what it was.

"'We no longer need living beings to manufacture our sustenance,' said the male. 'We are masters of all flesh now, and could alter ourselves if we wished it, so that we might eat any and every food—but we are what we are, and this is the nourishment for which nature and history shaped us.'

"He let some out into a goblet, and drank it, so that I should be certain what he meant, and what he was—but he did not offer the cup to me. There was no renewal of my former horror. I knew now what kind of a world I was in, and I understood. My hosts indicated that I should seat myself on a low sofa, and I complied. They apologized for the awkwardness of the conversation which I had had with the disembodied head, explaining that—as I had already deduced—it was a mere simulacrum of a living being, a machine whose capacity for action was limited. They went on to explain a great deal more.

"I learned that the spies set to watch for me were tiny machines of a very cheap and endlessly patient kind, which represented no considerable investment of effort. Even so, it was an effort which only a handful of persons out of the billions who dwelt on the earth thought worthwhile, and the machines had been designed in such a way that I might be brought to people who might be able to speak with me, rather than taking me to some public place where I might be paraded before crowds and exhibited as the marvel I undoubtedly was.

"They explained to me very earnestly that my species had long ago given way to a higher and better one, according to the dictates of the ineluctible laws of evolution, and was now known only by fragmentary relics. They assured me, however, that there had been no war of conquest, in which their kind had risen up against and defeated mine. According to their account, the human race had destroyed its own civilization, and all-but-obliterated its own heritage in a long series of increasingly-destructive wars, which had blasted apart

THE HUNGER AND ECSTASY OF VAMPIRES

the legacy of the Industrial Revolution even before that revolution had attained its climax. Everything mankind had built was destroyed, in the space of little more than a century.

"Their grasp of our chronology was a little vague, but they believed that the chain of disasters began in the twentieth century and was complete by the end of the twenty-first. After that, they said, there were no calendars left to chronicle the disastrous decline of once-civilized men into utter barbarity. According to their judgment, the intellectual flowering of our race had been hardly less brief than the life of a mayfly; *their* civilization, by contrast, had lasted for more than ten thousand years.

"I accepted this news with perfect equanimity, and did not doubt *then* that I was being told the truth. What they were saying—that humanity had destroyed itself, reduced itself to a savage existence *before* the overmen had restored the march of progress—did not seem in the least incredible while I bathed in that purple light, listening to the susurrus of the blood which swirled in the ornamental fountain. I understood that the civilization which provided men of my kind with all the rewards of comfort had been a very fragile thing, because the division of manual and intellectual labour which made factory production and scientific progress possible had robbed *individual* men of the elementary knowledge which would be essential to survival were the support of the complex productive system of modern society ever to fail.

"So muted had my own incredulity become that I was not surprised when my hosts told me that they would have the utmost difficulty persuading their contemporaries that I really had visited their world.

THE HUNGER AND ECSTASY OF VAMPIRES

"'You cannot begin to understand,' the male told me, 'how incredible it is that we are sitting in our own home, conversing with a ghost from the remotest antiquity. No one now believes in the reality of ghosts; we have long since cast such superstitions aside. It will be very difficult indeed to persuade our contemporaries that your appearance here is not some kind of cunning deception on our part. The machines we use nowadays are so very clever in manufacturing appearances that there is no conceivable proof we could offer that you really are what you seem to be. Indeed, we are acutely aware of the possibility that you are a hoax perpetrated upon us by malicious acquaintances.'

"'I am real,' I said, oddly helpless in the face of his apparent need for reassurance. 'I wish I could prove it to you.' But he looked at me so strangely that I knew I could not—that so far as he knew, this really might be a practical joke.

"'Can you possibly imagine,' he said, very softly, 'how little has survived into our world from yours? It is not merely the passage of time which has erased the record of your civilization—for I assure you that our archaeologists have been very assiduous in preserving every shard and fragment they could find—but the extremes of destruction achieved by your own wars. We know only a little more about your nineteenth century than we do about periods two or three thousand years earlier. We have less than a thousand texts written in the language we are now speaking, and almost all of them are incomplete.'

"I could not help but think of Shelley's poem about the ancient emperor whose shattered statue rested half-buried in a sea of sand, vainly bidding its discoverers to look upon his works and despair.

THE HUNGER AND ECSTASY OF VAMPIRES

"'What are you?' I whispered. 'How did it come about that *your* kind became lords of the earth, feeding on the blood of men like me?'

"He was enthusiastic to persuade me that I ought not to think of his ancestors as evil creatures. He was anxious to emphasize that it was to his ancestors that the descendants of mankind owed their survival. Had men not been domesticated, he said, the race would have become extinct—and when I protested that all the things which made us *men* had indeed been extinguished, he reminded me that there still remained a possibility that our ultimate descendants might once again become sentient, in a future as remote from his present as his era was from mine. If that came to pass, he said, those new men would reckon his kind the saviours of mankind instead of its destroyers.

"'It is the law of life,' said the female. 'New species emerge, achieve dominance, and are superseded in their turn.'

"'As you, too, will no doubt be superseded,' I said, with neither irony nor bitterness.

"She shook her head. 'Not so,' she said. 'There is an end to the sequence, when a species becomes master of its own evolution, by obtaining direct technical control over the hereditary material. Your species came very close to attaining such control, but your descendants destroyed the civilization they had built before they were able to make use of what they had learned.'"

"'And you can be perfectly certain that yours will not do likewise, I suppose,' I said.

"'I do not mean to insult you,' she assured me, "but my kind is better than yours. We are considerably more rational, and much less violent. We are not warlike by nature, and we have far less capacity for hatred than your kind had. What we have built we will certainly keep, and our mastery of the earth's biosphere is so complete that we can never be replaced. As you have seen, we have long since ceased to be dependent on the foodstuffs supplied to us by men, and we have adapted ourselves so that we are able to walk abroad in daylight quite comfortably—although we naturally still prefer the night-time.'

"They went on to tell me about the origins of their own kind. They admitted that their remote ancestors were predators who fed on the blood of mammals, including humans, but denied that they were vampires of the kind which featured so luridly in human folklore. They dismissed as mere superstitious nonsense the idea that their ancestors had been evil spirits which took possession of human corpses. Theirs, they said, was a natural species which lived invisibly on the margins of human society by virtue of its powers of mimicry. When I objected that their eyes would make it impossible for them to pass for men, even in the darkness which they favoured over daylight, they assured me that they could alter far more than the shape and colour of their pupils—and they proved their point.

"I have not taken the trouble to describe either of these individuals in any great detail, because their most distinctive features had made other differences seem trivial. The female had not appeared to me to be unusually pretty or unusually ugly by human standards, simply because there was little in her face which could command my attention save for her peculiar complexion and her disconcerting eyes. When she began to change, however, she first exerted herself to become more attractive—at least by human standards.

"The green light in her eyes faded, and the pupils became rounded, set in dark brown irises. The lustre of her flesh faded, and the paleness of her skin suddenly seemed much more ordinary. A few faint blemishes appeared, seemingly at random—but at the same time, she became startlingly beautiful. Her cheekbones shifted, and the lines of her face became more distinct; her eyebrows grew darker and her eyelashes longer. The changes were subtle, and yet quite devastating.

"She laughed delightedly when she saw my reaction. 'So I can do it,' she said, as though she had not dared to believe it. 'What an atavism I am! Is this truly the lure that my foremothers used for the seduction of human brutes?'

"They went on to explain that mimicry of this sort was a talent they had almost lost in the period of their first ascendancy, and that none among them really knew how adeptly their forebears used it—but that since they had learned the mechanisms which controlled all their bodily faculties, they had recovered the art and carried it to new extremes.

'Our minds have much greater authority over our bodies than yours,' the male said, 'for which reason we have no disease, and easily repair injuries which would be sufficient to kill one of you. Watch!'

"The woman began to change again, and this time far more ambitiously. I watched emotionlessly as her skin coarsened and became hairy, as her nose was elongated into a snout, as her hands changed into paws and her legs shrivelled. She completed the transformation into the appearance of a huge wolf, but began to change back almost immediately. As soon as her face was once again capable of bearing a smile she grinned very broadly. She clearly felt very pleased with herself.

"I took the appropriate inference readily enough; I understood what various means her remote ancestors had used to capture their prey, and why the only record of their existence which existed in the nineteenth century was a mere whisper of legend, heavily polluted by nightmarish fantasy. I understood the awful truth—and the hidden danger which lurked unseen in my own world."

* * * *

13

Copplestone paused to make sure that we were following the thread of his argument. If he was anxious lest tiredness should have led our thoughts astray he need not have worried. Even the frail and irritable Mr. Wells was rapt with attention.

It was Oscar Wilde who took the trouble to say what must have been on the mind of everyone in the room. "If what you are telling us is true, Professor," he said, laconically, "then the ancestors of these overmen must be alive today, hidden in the midst of human society. There might be one of them within this very company, holding his breath in fear of discovery."

He made a show of looking around, to see if anyone were indeed holding his breath.

"They would believe it readily enough in the country of my birth," the naturalized American opined, "and doubtless in yours, Count. Indeed, I know communists who think that all aristocrats are bloodsucking vampires. We are wiser than that, I hope."

"Was there not a tale put about regarding a soldier who served in Paris during the Commune?" asked the doctor's grey-eyed friend, softly. "A Sergeant Bertrand, was it not? Do you recall the case, Count?"

THE HUNGER AND ECSTASY OF VAMPIRES

"Why should I recall it?" I answered, coolly. "It was last year that I was in Paris, not half a lifetime ago. Was this sergeant a vampire, then?"

"The reports were unclear," the grey-eyed man replied, in deadly earnest. "He may have been a werewolf, or a ghoul— but the Protean nature of the accusation would not be inappropriate, if he really were a member of some predatory semi-human species like the one the Professor has described."

"If we are to proceed any further tonight," his companion interrupted him, "then I think we must get on— although I still believe that it would be wiser to stop. Ned, my friend, you really are not well enough to exert yourself this way."

Copplestone smiled, very wanly. He seemed to me to be on the point of collapse. Nevertheless, he continued his story, beginning at exactly the point at which he had left off.

"'So your ancestors were not merely vampires but also werewolves,' I said to my hosts. 'It is a wonder that you did not rule the world long before my own day. Or were the rumours of your invulnerability greatly exaggerated?'

"'Not so very greatly,' said the male. 'The crude shapeshifting abilities our ancestors had were associated with considerable powers of self-repair as well as virtually immunity to all disease, but....how well do you understand the mechanisms of evolution?'

"'I understand the theory of natural selection very well,' I told him, perhaps more haughtily than I was entitled to do. 'I met Charles Darwin fourteen years ago, a year before he died, and I discussed the implications of his theory with him.' After I had said that, of course, I realised that I might easily have given away the information I had determined to keep secret when the face on the flying machine's screen had tried to discover my point of origin, but it no longer seemed important—and in any case, the vampire did not react to Darwin's name.

"'In that case,' he said, 'you will understand that in the economics of evolution there is a correlation between lifespan and reproductive fecundity. Most natural species invest almost all of their energy in profligate reproduction, because it is easier for an organism to give birth to a thousand egg-cells, some few of which will survive to become new self-reproducing individuals, than it is to preserve the existing individuals against all the destructive pressures of the environment. At the same time, however, evolution has gradually produced organisms which are far more long-lived because of the reproductive advantages of parental care. Humans invest a far greater proportion of their energy in self-repair and self-preservation than most lower organisms, but they are only able to do so because of the protective care which they devote to the very few offspring they produce. I dare say that you can easily see the benign circularity of the argument, and can therefore appreciate that the species destined to replace mankind would be even longer-lived *but would produce even fewer offspring.*

"'For several hundred thousand years, while humans lived as hunter-gatherers, their total numbers were stable, and the number of my ancestors steadily increased. But when humans underwent the spectacular population explosion which followed the discovery of agriculture, and which continued exponentially—in spite of the limitations of disease—until the beginning of what you call the twenty-first century, my ancestors were ill-equipped by nature to keep up. Although their absolute numbers continued to increase, they did so very slowly, and it was not until the catastrophic fall of the fragile human empire that my own ancestors were enabled to emerge from hiding and claim their birthright.'

"I regretted my boastfulness regarding my understanding of the logic of evolution, because there were certain features of this argument I had the utmost difficulty grasping, but its general outline seemed clear enough. I understood that in my own time, the species known to us only through fancy-polluted tales of vampires and werewolves had been rare, because they multiplied so slowly by comparison with human beings—and although they were much less vulnerable to disease and injury than humans, they were by no means immortal.

"On repeating this to myself, I realised that I had acquired information which might be of incalculable value, provided only that the future which I had contrived to see was a future of *contingency* rather than a future of *destiny*. If I could warn my fellow men of the fate which awaited them, I thought, and prompt them to take action against the race that was waiting to enslave them, their reduction to the hideously ignominious status which I had glimpsed during my first expedition might yet be avoided.

"'I believe I know what you are thinking,' said the female, then. 'But I urge you to remember that *were it not for my kind, yours would have become extinct.* If you really are what you claim to be, you must abandon all thought of alerting your fellows to the presence in their midst of my kind. At best, they would think you mad; at worst, you might make certain the extinction of all intelligent life on earth.'

"'But our kind *will* triumph,' added the male, 'for are we not here?' He, evidently, believed in the future of destiny—

but how, I wondered, could he believe otherwise, even if his world *were* no more than a phantom of contingency? He could hardly be expected to accept the unflattering possibility that he, the history that had made him and the entire cosmos which contained him were mere figments of my imagination, although it was a possibility which seemed perfectly plausible to me.

"'That is not important,' said the female, who seemed to favour a different strategy of persuasion. 'You must understand, Copplestone, that the only hope for the future of your species rests with ours. We are masters of nature now, and it is in our power to make of mankind what we will. What you saw today in the forest is but one more chapter in a continuing story, and there may yet be a new ascent of man to sentience and civilization.'

"Why, I wondered, was she so anxious to make me concede this point? It was then, for the first time, that I wondered whether I might have been mesmerized, and that my two generous hosts might be exerting themselves to impress some kind of command upon my dulled mind.

"'No!' I said. 'I will not.....'

"At that precise moment in time, however, my timeshadow began to fade out, and I felt myself slipping away from that peculiar discussion into darkness.

"'No!' cried the male. 'You must not go! Please stay! There is so much more we have to say, so much more we need to learn....Stay, I beg of you!' He did not seem to realise that I had not the least control over the duration of my stay. He must have thought that my departure was a voluntary retreat and a calculated betrayal—but there was nothing I or anyone could do.

"I awoke, and found the doctor beside me, anxiously assisting me to wakefulness. I was, I fear, in a parlous state...."

THE HUNGER AND ECSTASY OF VAMPIRES

It seemed that the memory of that parlous state was sufficient to recall it, for even as he spoke he began to perspire very freely, and the tremor in his hands grew into a convulsion which shook his whole body. The empty brandy-glass slipped from his hand and shattered.

Although he tried with all his might to remain where he was, Copplestone slid from the chair on to the carpet, his body folding up into a quasi-foetal position. The doctor and the curly-haired young man both sprang to his aid, but they could not straighten him out, let alone deliver him from the fit which had possessed him.

So completely had the professor's narrative captivated me that I could not help but wonder whether this might be the wrath of the unborn inhabitants of an unmade future, recoiling from the uncertain mists of time to strike at the man who threatened the very possibility of their existence. It was absurd, I knew, but what a marvellous absurdity it was! I understood, then what Oscar Wilde meant by his ostentatious praise of gaudy lies. How poor a thing it was that common men took for common sense and common knowledge! How narrow a vision it afforded them, how meagre and inadequate a meal!

In that instant, at least, I wanted *everything* that Copplestone had said to be true. I desired with all my heart to be part of a crucial moment in the history of this world and the million futures which might conceivably proceed from it. I longed to forget my petty embarrassments and heartaches, and to set aside the awful power which *names* had to disturb and injure me.

It cannot possibly be a tissue of petty lies, I told myself. *What an adventure the man has had! Even if it has wrecked* him, body and soul, has it not been worth it? What traveller has ever had such a fine tale to tell? It should be true. It must be true.

* * * *

14

In time, Copplestone's fit passed. It was not anything the doctor did that eased the condition; it simply ran its course. When it had done so, Copplestone was unconscious, but peaceful.

In the meantime, I had arrived at certain conclusions, and made certain decisions. From that moment on, whatever the destiny of the world might be, mine was set in stone. I knew exactly what I intended to do, and how jealously I must guard the secret of my intention.

"I am very sorry," the doctor said. "I think you have all realised how desperate Professor Copplestone was to communicate the whole of his story to you in the space of a single night, but I do not think there is the least possibility of his being able to continue. He must be allowed to sleep, and recover himself. Perhaps I might suggest that any of you who have no other engagements—any of you, that is, who are sufficiently interested—might care to return here at eight o'clock tomorrow, so that the professor can acquaint you with the substance of his third...I dare not say *expedition*, although that is the word he would probably prefer....shall we say his third *vision*?"

I could not find it in my heart to admire his pedantic caution. He was not a fool, but he was blind to the riches of Copplestone's achievement. They all were—even the most brilliant of them. The men of letters could only see it as a bold fiction, the men of science as a wild farrago of superstitions. I was the only one who saw *hope* in it.

There was, inevitably, a certain amount of embarrassment and confusion in the company, although everyone present had in the end to agree that what the doctor proposed was the best possible solution. The manservant was summoned, and he and the doctor removed Copplestone to his bedroom while the rest of us made preparations for our departure.

The pale young man no longer seemed so excitable now, and the hectic flush had long since faded from his features. He seemed a trifle dispirited; I guessed that however his own oracular vision had proceeded, it was evidently not in any direction similar to what he had just heard. The two men of science had already begun conversing in hurried whispers, while the other young man and the doctor's taciturn companion were staring deep into the glowing embers of Copplestone's fire, lost in problematic contemplation.

"Well," Wilde said to me, not quite *sotto voce*, "we have had our money's worth, have we not? And a good supper too! What a magnificent fantasist the man is! If only he had not told us of his long experiments with mind-addling drugs I would immediately have proclaimed him a genius, but I fear that he has relied too much on the power of chemical hallucination to be given all the credit for his accomplishments. Even so, it is a fabulous tale—a truly fabulous tale! I wish I had the courage to steal it, but the altercation between our host and young Mr. Wells makes me wary of the consequences of such a theft. Still, it might be worth doing, given that the deftness of *my* hand could improve it out of all recognition...."

"Be careful, Oscar," I said, making a feeble attempt to mimic his witty manner of speech. "You might start a new fashion, and then where would we be? Every Tom, Dick and Harry would be producing visions of the future. Within a dozen years we'd have a thousand different fever-dreams to choose from."

"True," he said. "Probably best to leave such things to that sot Griffith-Jones and young Mr. Wells—that way the fad will surely die stillborn."

As we bustled about putting on our coats and hats the conversation continued in a muted but not unfriendly fashion. Apart from myself only the British scientist had brought his own carriage, and when this became clear he and I swiftly became adamant that we could accommodate all our fellow guests in our spare seats, thus saving them the trouble—which might have been considerable at that hour—of summoning hansoms or risking the terrors of the underground railway.

Upon comparing destinations it became obvious that the most convenient use of resources would be for the two young men of letters to travel with the two men of science, while Wilde and I played host to the doctor and the grey-eyed man. The physician and his dour companion were headed for Baker Street, which was very near, and only a little out of my way given that I had then to deliver Wilde to his selected home-from-home. For my own part, I resolved to pay a short visit to Piccadilly before going to the house I had rented.

There was some delay while the doctor convinced himself that Copplestone could safely be left to the care of his servants, and in the end he had to hurry out to the carriage, where his friend had already taken his seat. I tried to dismount, for politeness' sake, but the doctor—who was fumbling at his buttons—cannoned into me and dropped his bag. We both bent to pick it up, and collided yet again.

I took advantage of the confusion to pluck the envelope containing Copplestone's formula out of his jacket, as neatly as the best pickpocket in Paris, and I slipped it unobtrusively into my coat.

As soon as we were under way, I asked the doctor what he thought of Copplestone's remarkable adventures.

"I must reserve my judgment," he said. "I have made the man a promise, and must keep it. But I'll say this much—if he cannot be persuaded to give up this damnable drug, I fear for his very life. He does not know—or will not understand—how ill he is."

"And you, sir?" I asked his friend—who had hardly said a word all evening, so far as I knew. "What is your opinion?"

He looked at me very steadily with his solemn grey eyes. "It is the strangest tale I have ever heard," he said, gravely. "If one were to accept its truth, if only as a momentary hypothesis, it would raise many interesting questions and a host of curious possibilities. But I pride myself on my scrupulous use of logic, and I would find it difficult to accept the reality of the art of prophecy without firmer proof. I suppose it would be easier by far to believe that it was the record of a sequence of hallucinations....but I would be interested to hear *your* opinion of what we have heard."

"I hardly know what to make of it," I said, in a calculatedly off-hand manner. "I fear that I have neither Wilde's love of fabulation nor Mr. Wells' intense interest in the distant future of mankind—and I must admit that I had great difficulty following parts of the narrative. English is not my first language, you know."

"Nor, I think, is French," said the doctor's friend, "although your accent has far more of Paris in it than echoes of your native land, and your clothes were purchased there. Some of your consonants sound Slavic, but whatever its origin might really be, Lugard is certainly not a Slavic name. Your coachman is unmistakably Bavarian, of course. I have known only one other man with a physiognomy similar to yours, and he claimed to be Russian—unfortunately, his name and title proved to be false, and I never did manage to ascertain his true origins. Like yourself, he was an uncommonly fastidious man, who took little or no pleasure in food and wine, and found tobacco smoke distasteful."

I was not at all amused by this remarkable speech, which seemed more than slightly insulting, and in any case implied that I had been closely observed during the course of the evening without my realising the fact. It was on the tip of my tongue to say that I hoped he did not suspect my name and title of being false, but I knew only too well that one should never tempt fate in such a fashion.

"I say, old friend," said the doctor, uncomfortably, "this isn't one of my infernal stories, you know." He, at least, was fully aware of the fact that acceptance of the hospitality of my carriage carried a certain burden of obligation.

"It is ingrained in the nature of Englishmen to dislike everything foreign," observed Wilde, with mocking disingenuity. "You would not think an Irishman a particularly exotic creature, but everyone in England seems to think me a specimen fit for the Zoological Gardens. I fear, Count, that

THE HUNGER AND ECSTASY OF VAMPIRES

you will find many people in London who are morbidly fascinated by the fact that you hail from somewhere east of Calais."

"I meant no offence!" protested the doctor's friend, with all apparent sincerity. "I fear that careful observation of everyone I meet has become a constant preoccupation which I cannot easily abandon for politeness' sake. I am curious, merely curious. I really would like to know what you thought of Dr Copplestone's adventure, Count Lugard."

"After all," Wilde chipped in again, "your opinion as an authentic man of the world is worth a great deal. There is not an Englishman in existence with sufficient romance in his blood to appreciate the story we were told tonight, and I fear that the adoptive American—who is, like all adoptive Americans, trying very hard indeed to be utterly and completely American—is listening with an organic instrument which can only pay attention to matters of electricity and gadgetry. Even the young man from the Caribbean found his attention deflected by his friend's anxiety over the apparent borrowing of his ideas."

"You are, as usual Oscar, quite unjust," I said to him—truthfully enough. "The young man with the high-pitched voice evidently has a soul overfull of romance, and Sir William Crookes is broadminded enough to place equal credence in cathode rays and ghosts. As for Copplestone, who is surely as English as Stonehenge....who could possibly charge him with a lack of romance? The man is an amateur storyteller, to be sure—but what a story he tells!"

"For all its bizarrerie," Wilde said, "the narrative lacks colour, wit and action. Were I to tell the tale, how much finer it would be....oh, the temptation!"

THE HUNGER AND ECSTASY OF VAMPIRES

"It is a perfectly fascinating tale," I retorted, taking care to sound insincere. "Perhaps I have not your refined aesthetic sensibilities, and perhaps I am the worse for it, but I find Copplestone's vision of the future quite entrancing."

As I spoke these words I glanced at the doctor's friend, challenging him to read the truth of my remarks.

The grey-eyed man said simply: "We will doubtless learn tomorrow whether the human race is to be regenerated thirty thousand years or more from today. I would like to think so—I find Mr. Wells' anticipation of a dark, dead world so very bleak."

"Young men often dally with an extreme bleakness of outlook," said Wilde. "They think it romantically interesting. In fact, it is merely the measure of their own cowardice in the face of the stings and darts of outrageous fortune. If they are fortunate, they learn to grasp life's nettle. If not, they gradually transform themselves into pusillanimous old men weighed down by acrid regret—and need no shapeshifting gift to accomplish the metamorphosis."

I thought that the doctor shot him a darkly resentful glance, but he said nothing.

"The real point, of course," the grey-eyed man put in, "is not what will happen thousands of years in the future, but what will happen tomorrow and the day after that. Whatever the action of Copplestone's drug is, it is a very remarkable compound which will repay further study. We may dare to hope that its discovery might be a great boon to mankind, even if it is nothing more than a manufacturer of vivid hallucinations."

"What could mankind possibly need more than a manufacturer of vivid hallucinations?" asked Oscar Wilde—but

THE HUNGER AND ECSTASY OF VAMPIRES

he was talking about himself, not Copplestone's formula.

"Here is Baker Street," I said to the grey eyed-man, with scrupulous mildness. "Tell me when you want to be set down, and I'll alert the coachman."

"Anywhere above number two hundred will do," he replied, as if he were wary of telling me the precise address.

Our *au revoirs* were polite enough, but a trifle frosty.

* * * *

15

"Forgive them, dear boy," said Wilde, once we were under way once again, "for they know not what they are. A consulting detective, indeed! I am by no means devoid of conceit, as you know, but such a frail delusion must be very difficult to entertain! And yet the doctor is as famous a literary man, in his way, as I am. *The Strand* has a huge circulation, the envy of all its competitors and imitators." He sounded more than a little envious himself— he was never a man to conceal his deadly sins.

"As Copplestone rightly says," I observed, sympathetically "there are so many periodicals these days."

"But the only ones really worth reading are in French," he said, mournfully. "Even Lane's *Yellow Book* is conspicuously thin-blooded. I wish it were not so difficult to obtain the *Mercure* in London. Now *there* one may find dreams which have delicacy of form as well as bravery of vision. The best French writers always display an appropriate nicety, even when they treat such brutal themes as vampirism. The French vampires of Nodier and Gautier are far more beguiling than their English kin."

"Are there any English vampires?" I asked.

"Not so very many," he replied. "In prose, there has been little more than that ludicrous excrescence of Polidori's that he tried to pass off as Byron's, and the interminable penny-dreadful adventures of the appalling Varney. Le Fanu's 'Carmilla' is infinitely better than either, but le Fanu is yet another graduate of Trinity, like Stoker—and hence not really English, like myself. Stoker, I believe, is enthusiastically researching the history and folklore of vampirism, so that he might write another 'Carmilla'. If he carries through his intention—and he is nothing if not assiduous—the literary world will doubtless have its due ration of Anglo-Irish vampires. You will not understand this, being a civilized man of the world, but Trinity is a Protestant college in the heart of a Catholic country, built on an ancient cesspit, and it provides uncommonly fertile ground for the growth of feverish tales of exotic outsiders. The Anglo-Irish sometimes think themselves more English than the English, because they have to strive so hard to avoid being Irish, but the English will never support our pretence—they insist that we are outsiders even more firmly than the Irish do."

I could not fully appreciate the bitter undercurrent of feeling which underlay this flippant commentary, but the mention of Stoker recalled to my mind the fact that Copplestone had thought of inviting him to hear the story he had just related. Wilde's revelation that Stoker might be thinking of writing a vampire story might provide the explanation of that fact, but I was by no means happy to learn it. What unfortunate inspiration, I wondered, might Arminius Vambery have communicated to the man?

"Do you know anything about this project of Stoker's?" I asked.

Wilde shrugged. He had turned his face away, as though to look out of the window of the carriage. "Not a great deal," he said. "I told you earlier—we were close once, but we no longer see one another."

"Oh yes," I murmured, without thinking. "You once liked his wife."

"Loved," said Wilde, acidly. "I would have married her myself, but for being haunted by the twin spectres of poverty and the pox. And now....." He trailed off.

I was amazed that he said so much. He was tired, and he had had more than a little to drink, but even a man as naturally garrulous as he would surely never have said such a thing in the normal course of conversation with a man he hardly knew. It was not difficult, though, to follow the abandoned line of argument. *An Ideal Husband* had been running for a week and *The Importance of Being Earnest* was in rehearsal. Wilde was set fair for great fame and fortune, and his future was surely brighter by far than Stoker's, whatever their comparative prospects had been ten or twenty years ago. As for fear of the pox, if he meant by that what I thought he meant then he must have laid that particular ghost by the time he married Constance Lloyd. Conventional wisdom, I knew, taught that a man diagnosed with syphilis must take the mercury treatment and suffer two years abstinence from sexual intercourse—although I had my doubts, personally, as to whether the mercury treatment had any more effect on that disease than poor Jean Lorrain's blood-supping and ether-swilling had had on his.

"Oscar," I said, on impulse, "I fear that I may not be able to remain in London very long."

"Why is that?" he asked.

"Because certain rumours will doubtless follow me, in time, from Paris. I think your friend Stoker might have heard them already, and he is sure to repeat them if he discovers that I am here—and I fear that the man who just left us is not the only man in London afflicted by infernal curiosity. One such as he would easily root the rumours out, if he had the inclination to try."

"I wish I could say that I never listen to rumours," said Wilde, carelessly, "but you know perfectly well that I always do. I am the subject of so many, and although I pretend to like it....as it happens, I am thinking of going away myself. A clairvoyante I know has foretold that I shall make a pilgrimage to Algeria, and now I have Copplestone's assurance that such prophecies ought to be taken seriously I dare not flout my destiny. Perhaps you ought to come with us."

"Us?" I queried.

"I could not think of going alone to such an uncivilized place," he said, "and poor Bosie is so cut up about Drumlanrig's death. His brother, you know. Even Queensberry liked Drumlanrig, a little."

"I never go so far south," I told him. "I cannot abide the sun, and its light is so horribly fierce in those latitudes. I like London's grey light much better, and I shall be very sorry to leave."

"You might stand fast against the rumour-mongers," he suggested, mildly. "Let them say what they like, and be damned—or haul them into court for libel. Either would be better than a shooting-match, don't you think?"

I looked at him long and hard, wondering how much he knew—and how much he cared.

"Sometimes," I murmured, "I wish that poor Mourier had fired at my heart, and found his mark."

"But only sometimes," said Wilde, with patient understanding. "We all think ourselves monsters, occasionally—but once we look away from the stubbornly unflattering mirror, there is the world awaiting us, in all its welcoming glory. If nothing else, a tale like Copplestone's puts our petty woes into their proper perspective, does it not? A thousand years hence, you and I and all our world will be mere dust, not even a memory—and no one will know or care what we were, or what we did, or even what we wrote. Let us to our playground, my friend, to amuse ourselves while we may. We'll be long enough dead, when the time comes."

I wished that I could take matters so lightly, and bring such eloquence to the cure of my own heart's sickness, but he and I were not the same kind of man.

"Shall I pick you up tomorrow?" I asked him, as he got down from the carriage.

"I would not miss it for the world," he assured me. "The same time, the same place. I promise that I shall not be late."

Of all his promises, that was worth the least.

* * * *

16

It was so late by the time my faithful Bavarian set me down in Piccadilly that the vast majority of the night-birds had returned to their roosts, but I knew by now that the street never quite died, even on the coldest and foggiest of nights. Tonight the fog was very slight indeed; there was nothing but a few stray wisps of mist drifting about the gas-lamps, seemingly gathered there for the sake of the yellow light. The raucous music which spilled from the closed doors of the all-night drinking-dens was muffled only by the doors and curtains set firm to keep the winter cold at bay.

I found the particular night-bird I sought at her station beneath one of the wrought-iron lamp standards. She smiled as she saw me approach.

She was very pale, and her pallor bore the subtly lustrous bloom which was an infallible sign of consumption. She made no attempt to cover it with powder; there was no real need, for the smallpox which had visited her in youth as it visited all the city's poorer children had left but a single visible scar on her face: an oddly star-like mark on the cheek beneath the left eye.

Her dark eyes were bright, seemingly almost luminous by virtue of the way they caught the lamplight. She had lovely hair, which she kept in very neat trim, and to look at its careful arrangement one might have thought that she had only just descended to the street.

"My Russian Count," she said, as I halted before her. Her voice was low and her pronunciation perfect. I had first been attracted to her as much by her voice as her features; I could not abide dropped aitches and revolting pet-names, and could never understand why so many English whores took such a pride in Cockney vulgarity.

I took her hand in mine, and raised it momentarily towards my lips, although I did not complete the gesture. The hand was very cold.

"You should not stand outside for such long periods," I said, hypocritically. "On a night like this you should retreat indoors, as your sisters do, and place yourself near a blazing fire."

I was at least partly responsible for her chill. She had chosen to remain outdoors because she was waiting for me, although she had no reason to believe that I would come to her tonight—or ever again. She was bound to wait for me, by virtue of the mesmeric spell I had put on her when first we met.

"Will you walk with me, my dear," I said, and she nodded, although not very eagerly.

We strolled off in the direction of Green Park, whose Stygian darkness obligingly provided a curtain to mask the most elementary commerce of the district. Her lack of enthusiasm was easy enough to understand; the ground would be iron-hard and icy, and she had every right to expect greater comfort from a man of my station. She might have objected, but that would have taken a little more courage than she had.

THE HUNGER AND ECSTASY OF VAMPIRES

In fact, she had nothing to fear. I had not the slightest intention of taking her into the darkness and laying her down upon the turf. I escorted her along the pavement to a spot equidistant between two of the street-lights. I had no difficulty in making out her features, but she must have been nearly blind to mine. I looked long into her eyes, but it is a cliché of cheap fiction which says that a mesmerist must use the authority of his gaze, and it was it more for my sad and sombre pleasure than to extend my dominion over her spirit.

I knew that I had only to stroke her cheek a little, and fold my protective arms round her, to make her completely mine.

"Oh my love!" she murmured. It was not a trick of the trade. Perhaps she did speak softly to more casual acquaintances—perhaps she used those very words—but there was no dissimulation in her voice now.

"There is something you must do for me," I whispered, my lips just a breath away from her delicate ear. "I believe that you have the cunning for it. It should not be difficult—the manservant has no company in the house save for his master and the crone who is mistress of the kitchen."

"Anything," she said, almost imperceptibly. She wanted nothing other than to be my slave. How could she?

I pressed a sovereign into her hand, but had to close her nerveless fingers around it to make sure that she held on to it.

"There will be more," I said. "Do this for me, and I will give you everything that is within my power to give." There was hypocrisy in this, too, but there was a kind of honesty too. For once—perhaps for the first time in my life—there was a measure of substance in my seductive promises.

"Tomorrow," I told her, "I will take you home with me. It may be late when I come, but I *will* come. Trust me, Laura. Trust me."

"My name..." she began—but I put a finger to her lips to silence her.

"Your name," I told her, "is Laura. It has always been, and always will be Laura."

She had tilted her head back, neck bared in that curious instinctive gesture of submission which civilized humans somehow retain: the purely animal gesture of surrender, which offers the throat to a conqueror as a demonstration of faith in the mercy of the strong.

Her name was Laura, and always would be. She accepted that. She was completely in my power.

The situation was familiar, but I was afflicted with an altogether unfamiliar uncertainty as to how it might proceed and develop. I felt that I simply could not go on any longer in the same deep rut—that I had no choice but to step aside from the path which had so far seemed to be my undeniable destiny. After all, had I not told Edward Copplestone that the only destiny was death—and implied without saying it that outside of death, *all* things might yet be possible?

I lowered my head slowly, and kissed my darling very gently on the throat, to seal our pact.

* * * *

17

Needless to say, Wilde was not ready when I arrived—exactly at the appointed hour—to collect him. By way of apology he explained that he had been run ragged all day, in a hopeless attempt to catch up with his belated start. I deduced from his sketchy explanations that the rehearsal itself had not gone awry, but that something else was amiss: something he did not care to spell out. I took the inference that he had seen Lord Alfred Douglas, and that the meeting had come to friction almost immediately. Wilde really did look tired, but it was an exhaustion of the spirit rather than the body—the kind of distress which creeps into the corners of a life which is lived to the full and then beyond.

I was anxious on his behalf; such lives as that sometimes fracture under the insidious stress, and fall apart. I wondered whether the day might soon come when he would feel as much need as I for the secret which I had stolen from Copplestone's doctor—but I dismissed the thought. I had suffered the corrosions of Vambery's slanders for many years; wherever I went there was at least one pair of catlike eyes in every crowd which stared at me from beneath lowered lids, and one pair of lips which whispered: "Impostor! Vampire!

Monster of depravity!" He was insulated from any such fate by his charm and his fame—and, above all else, by his genius. No panther in the world could drag him down and rake him with its claws, even though he was not in the least afraid to feast with their kind. He was tired now, but he would wake more fully than any common man; I was awake, but I had nightmares lying in wait for me every time I closed my eyes.

He saw me studying him, and roused himself; he had a reputation to maintain, even in the security of a carriage with no audience but a foreign friend.

"Irregular hours do not seem to disturb *you* in the least," he observed, with only the slightest hint of feigned resentment. "You could not have got to your bed before five last night, and yet you seem perfectly refreshed. By way of adding insult to injury you look ten years younger than I do, although I cannot believe that you are."

"Nonsense," I said, knowing full well that the last thing he wanted was a confirmation of the fact that I was older than he—although of course I was. "You are as handsome as ever, and now that night has fallen the gleam is returning to your own eyes. We are two of a kind, you and I; we only come to life after dark, when even the workers of the world must retreat from their toil to the world of thought and imagination: the world where truly *human* life is lived."

More hypocrisy, I thought, *more seduction.* But how could one possibly have a conscience about lying to a man who prized great lies far above the humble truth?

"All the workers of the world do not toil by day," he remarked, as my trusty Bavarian took advantage of a rare stretch of clear road to whip his team to a fast trot. "Actors work by limelight, and even playwrights sometimes find inspiration in what common men would call insomnia."

"That is not work," I said, "no matter that it is the means by which some men earn their coin. *Work* is what happens in the fields and in the factories, producing the bare necessities of life. Wheat and meat, clothing and shelter, are the means of physical survival; their production alone qualifies as authentic toil. The theatre belongs to the life of the mind, to the fabulous realm of luxury and whoredom which is merely the means by which men make life *worthwhile*."

He looked at me curiously, but did not smile, as I had hoped he might. Perhaps he felt insulted by my implication that what playwrights did was a kind of whoredom rather than a species of true labour. What he actually said, however, was: "Modern factories take no account of day or night. Machines do not care for the sun, or for sleep, but only for power—and because machines are blind and tireless, the men and women who attend them must work shift after shift around the clock. Perhaps it was young Wells, and not Ned Copplestone, who read the meaning of their common dream correctly. Perhaps the tribute of blood was in truth being paid to the machines themselves, not to the overseers whom Copplestone carelessly called vampires."

Wilde's was the fashionable socialism of the upper classes, scrupulously benevolent and safely abstracted from over-extravagant demonstration—but it was by no means insincere. He might have felt a deeper and more painful hatred of social injustice had he been apprenticed to a blacking factory or a draper's shop, but his vision could not be faulted on grounds of clarity.

"I had not thought to find you in such a serious mood," I said, half-apologetically. "I hoped that the anticipation of more gorgeous fabrications would have helped you to be gay."

He made a visible effort, then, to throw off his tiredness and the slight peevishness with which it had infected him.

"You are right, my friend," he said, "as you almost invariably are. We *are* two of a kind, despite that you are nobly born and I am not. We are true aristocrats of the mind and of the heart. Forgive me for envying your composure. Ever since I wrote the terrible parable of Dorian Gray I have become acutely conscious of the aging process, and there are times when I simply cannot help feeling old. My mind is brilliantly young, but my flesh...."

"I would readily trade my sturdy flesh for an artist's soul like yours," I told him.

He looked at me in the strangest way. "I once wrote a tale of a fisherman's soul," he said, "which was cast out to roam free, rather as Copplestone's soul has roamed, but was so corrupted in the process....oh, enough of this dour allegorization! Let us look forward; let us fix our minds on the remotest future, on the world of the overmen, whose mastery of nature has permitted the transcendence of all frailties. Tell me, Count, do you suppose that the gift of thought will be restored to poor, deprived humanity in Copplestone's third vision? Do you think that they might somehow turn the tables on their vampire conquerors?"

"The good should end happily and the bad unhappily," I quoted, casually. "That is what fiction means. But Copplestone so ardently desires to present us with truth and *not* fiction that he will surely disregard such elementary rules. No, I cannot believe that he will end his story as conventionally as that. I trust, however, that he has kept the best of his surprises up his sleeve, and that he will have something to reveal which none of us could possibly anticipate."

I permitted myself a private smile as I said it, thinking that there might be one surprise which I could anticipate— but I spoke more truly than I knew. Because of Wilde's tardiness we were the last to arrive at Copplestone's house, and because of that we were the last to learn of his death.

* * * *

18

We were shown into the dining-room, where the others awaited us. The table was not laid but they were all seated around it, very solemnly. The doctor had taken the place at the head of the table which Copplestone had occupied the night before, and he beckoned us impatiently to be seated. Apparently they had been waiting for us for some little time.

"This is terrible news," said Wilde. "How did it happen?" I, meanwhile, was wondering why we were taking our places, given that the man who was supposed to complete his story was no longer able to discharge that duty. Were we, perhaps, to undertake our planned discussion of the enigmas of destiny after all, as some kind of tribute to the dead man?

"I fear that Professor Copplestone, having fallen asleep last night, simply never woke up," said the doctor. "I had given his manservant an instruction that he was not on any account to be disturbed, and it was not until noon that he finally crept into his master's room and found him dead. He summoned me immediately. The body has been taken away to King's College Hospital, where a *post mortem* examination will be carried out, but I have no doubt of the cause of death. Professor Copplestone poisoned himself with his damnable drugs."

THE HUNGER AND ECSTASY OF VAMPIRES

"We cannot be absolutely certain where the responsibility lies," his friend put in. His tone was mild enough, but harboured a fugitive element of threat.

"Why should you doubt it, sir?" said Wilde, less sarcastically than he probably intended. "Surely you can't think that poor Copplestone was murdered?"

"If that were the case," said the Great Detective, soberly, "I doubt that we could ever prove it, given that he was so ready to take poison by his own hand. But he *was* robbed, and on that account I think we must reserve our judgment as to the precise manner of his death."

"Robbed?" said Wilde. "What was stolen?"

"The vial which he showed to us last night," the grey-eyed man reported. "The vial which he intended to offer to us, so that one of us might venture to confirm that his supposed visions of the future were accurate."

"But that surely cannot matter," I put in, smoothly. "Your friend the doctor still has the formula."

"I fear," said the doctor, blushing beneath his whiskers, "that I have not. As soon as I became aware of the theft from Copplestone's laboratory I checked my pocket, and found that the envelope had disappeared. There is no possibility that I could have dropped it accidentally; it must have been removed from my jacket by a thief, probably while it hung in the closet last night."

"That is not possible, old friend," his companion said. "Had someone entered our rooms, I can assure you that their visit would have left clear evidential traces. I know how reluctant you are to admit that your pocket might have been picked while you were fully awake and alert, but there is no doubt in *my* mind that that is exactly what happened."

THE HUNGER AND ECSTASY OF VAMPIRES

"But who would do such a thing?" asked Wells. "And why? It could not have been one of us, because any one of us could have had the contents of the vial for the asking—there was no need to steal it."

"Perhaps the thief did not care to compete with others for the privilege," said the detective, who clearly felt that he was now getting into his stride. In is own fashion, he was as anxious for an audience as Oscar Wilde.

"I doubt that the competition would have been fierce," said Sir William, drily. "Had the thief known that Copplestone lay dead in his bed, he could have been reasonably certain that there would be a dearth of volunteers."

"Perhaps the professor's worst fears were justified," I suggested, cynically. "Perhaps the vampires who rule the world whose secrets he penetrated did indeed contrive to find a way to reach back into time, so that they might cancel out his discovery, thus promoting their contingent future to the status of destiny. Perhaps we are all in deadly danger now that we have heard the story—or part of it, at any rate; I suppose there is no hope now of our hearing the rest."

"Not so," said Shiel. "It seems that we shall indeed hear the rest, at least in an abridged form. That is one reason why we have not dispersed, but waited for you and Mr. Wilde to join us."

"And what is the other reason?" asked Wilde.

This time, it was the grey-eyed man who answered. "It is not impossible that we may yet be able to shed some light on the mysteries of the stolen vial and the missing formula."

I could see that the would-be detective was doing his best to be diplomatic, but Wilde was not the only person

THE HUNGER AND ECSTASY OF VAMPIRES

present who bridled at the implication that we were all to be interrogated on suspicion of being thieves.

"Aha!" said Wilde, sourly. "So we are to have the privilege of watching the great detective at work! And will you, Mr. Shiel, be pitting *your* methods against his?"

It seemed that the curly-haired young man did not know whether to smile or frown, but I observed that the great detective was honestly puzzled.

"How did you know that...?" the young man began—but he stopped even before Wilde interrupted him, having divined that the answer was obvious.

"I have my methods too, dear boy," said Wilde, airily. "I have an indefatigable ear for gossip, and nothing that happens in the offices of John Lane escapes my notice. Every aspiring writer in London—with the possible exception of Mr. Wells—has been impressed by the awesome success of the doctor's reportage, and I dare say that you are not the only one to have a book of detective stories forthcoming, although I am quite positive that you are the only one to have modelled his detective on dear Count Stenbock."

"Count Stenbock!" exclaimed the doctor, incredulously.

"I merely tried to be true to the spirit of Poe," said the young man, disingenuously. "He, after all, is the true father of the detective story. If I have been a little fanciful....well, even the good doctor is fanciful in his own way."

He was interrupted by the fist of the grey-eyed man, which rudely called for order by rapping sharply upon the table. "This is a *serious matter*," he said, sternly. "Copplestone is dead, and the remainder of the drug which induced the remarkable dreams whose contents he confided to us last night has certainly been stolen. I accuse no one, and it is certainly not beyond the bounds of possibility that rumours of his achievements have escaped, in spite of his determination to quell them, but the fact remains that the only people who knew in any real detail what Copplestone believed he had discovered are here in this room. The doctor and I have questioned the servants, but my friend is quite sure, on the basis of his long acquaintance with Copplestone's household, that neither of them had any real idea of the nature of their master's work, and hence no evident motive for the theft."

"I cannot see that any of us had an *evident* motive," said the American. "There was nothing in what we heard last night to suggest that Copplestone's visions were anything more than mere delusion, and Mr. Wells gave us some reason to suspect that the delusion may have had a perfectly ordinary seed in something Copplestone had read or heard about."

"Quite so," I agreed, savouring my hypocrisy. "I cannot see that any one of us could have concluded that there might be *profits* to be made out of this drug, nor that any one of us would have been inspired to try to corner the market."

Tesla's eyes narrowed, but he said nothing. He was not sure whether or not I was insulting him by implication. In fact, of course, I was merely introducing a red herring into the discussion.

"As far as I can see," Wells put in—apparently in much the same spirit, though doubtless without any covert motive to compare with mine—"there are only two people in this room who had ample opportunity to seize both the vial and the formula. Has anyone here been to this house today, except for the doctor and his friend?"

"That," said the great detective, seemingly untroubled by the back-handed accusation, "is one thing we ought to ascertain."

Understandably, no one confessed to having visited the house. I assumed that no one had. I had not; there had been no need, when I could so easily send another in my stead.

"Are you quite certain, doctor," said Wilde, "that Copplestone never woke again after falling asleep last night? Is it possible that he got up and went to his laboratory? If it is, then he might have removed the vial himself. Perhaps he discarded the compound, having thought better of his offer to let us poison ourselves with it. Perhaps he quaffed it himself— surely it is possible, if not more than likely, that the contents of the vial provided the dose which killed him?"

The doctor considered the hypothesis. "I cannot prove that he never woke up again," he admitted. "And if, perchance, he did drink the contents of the vial....it could easily have killed him. I begged him not to increase the dose again following the second experiment, but he would not listen. As he came out of his coma for the last time he suffered a severe physical disturbance. I could not credit his own explanation of this phenomenon, and I think it not unlikely that Copplestone's brain had become permanently vulnerable to fits like the one which apparently killed him. Any dose, however small, might have finished him off."

"But we could not find the marked vial," the grey-eyed man pointed out. "It certainly was not beside him when he died. That suggests...."

"Excuse my interrupting," said Shiel, who was perhaps overkeen to find an opportunity to display his own instinct for detective work "but exactly what *was* this explanation which you could not credit, doctor?"

The doctor shook his head, but not in denial. "Copplestone imagined that he was somehow being *attacked*," he said, in a slightly uncomfortable tone. "He could not in the end shake off the suspicion he had formed while he was aboard the flying machine—while, that is, he *dreamed* that he was aboard the flying machine—that the face on the screen was urgently desirous of finding out where and when he came from in order that the men—*overmen*, that is—of the future might attempt to reach back into the past....just as Count Lugard has suggested, albeit in jest."

"Rumour has it that many a true word is spoken in jest," said Wilde, smoothly. "Perhaps the Count is right. Perhaps Copplestone *was* murdered by the inhabitants of a contingent future in order to prevent his setting in train the chain of causality which would have nipped the victory of the overmen in the bud and condemned their entire future history to the oblivion of non-existence. Perhaps we are *all* in danger."

"This is a complete waste of time," said Tesla. "If we are here to listen to the third part of Copplestone's story, then let's hear it. Otherwise, I for one intend to be on my way. I've no intention of sitting here while some amateur sleuth interrogates me as to my movements because he thinks I might be a thief."

"How is it, exactly," I enquired, curiously, "that we may hear the third part of the story, given that poor Copplestone is no longer alive to tell it?"

"I have discovered," said the doctor, "there is a *written* version of Copplestone's third dream, which he must have made almost immediately afterwards—as soon as I let him alone, in fact. His suspicions regarding the attempts which might be made by the people of the far future to prevent his publicising his discoveries, however absurd they may have been, were quite real. The accounts which he gave us verbally of his first two dreams were, of course, much fuller and more considered than this written version of his third dream, and I am certain that had he had the chance to tell the story himself he would have elaborated considerably upon it, but...."

"Oh, get on with it, man!" said Wilde, intemperately.

The doctor looked around for moral support, but there was little to be found, even from his friend. The majority opinion obviously agreed with Wilde. The doctor, somewhat shamefacedly, left the room to fetch the relevant document.

"Let us leave the matter of the theft to one side, for now," said the amateur detective, equably—exactly as if it were his own idea and his own decision to do so. I noticed, however, that when he said it his eyes were fixed on me.

I could not help but wonder what he might possibly have deduced or found out that inspired him to favour me with such a glance, but I told myself sternly that it was only coincidence, and I was very careful to meet his gaze without giving the least hint of any discomfiture.

* * * *

19

"You must remember," said the doctor, "that these documents were not intended for publication. They are, in effect, hurried *aides memoires* with a few supplementary notes of a very brief nature. There is doubtless much of Copplestone's experience that is omitted altogether or referred to only obliquely, and what passes for straightforward reportage is continually interrupted by comments, questions and what I can only describe as *philosophical rhapsodies*. The contents of the conversations which I had with Copplestone following his experiments provide a context which sometimes allows me to interpret his meaning a little more easily than an unprepared reader, but there is much herein which remains wholly mysterious to me."

In the privacy of my thoughts I echoed Wilde's admonition—but the doctor was ready at last, and he began to read.

"What confusion! What astonishment! I must be calm. I must at least *try* to make a sober and intelligible record. To put pen to paper is to diminish the experience ludicrously, perhaps to distort it utterly, but I must *try*.

THE HUNGER AND ECSTASY OF VAMPIRES

"The beginning. The hill again; the slope was not as steep, perhaps because of the erosions of wind and rain, perhaps due to an altogether arbitrary shift in the pattern of the land. The forest was very different: huge trees, far taller and straighter than anything known on earth in my own time; the foliage, seen from below, presented mixed colours ranging from turquoise to purple; the light which filtered through the canopy was subdued and bluish—presumably comfortable to the eyes of the overmen.

"The purpose of the forest may be—must be—to make the daylit world as comfortable a place for overmen as the world by night....but there were no overmen there, only machines. Machines everywhere! Tiny metal cells which were able to associate, as the golem did, in order to transform themselves into complex 'organisms'. What are the limits of their virtuosity? How many different kinds are there? Why did organic life not evolve according to this pattern, so that hordes of protozoans might come together to take whatever form might suit their temporary circumstances?

"Perhaps it did, for a while. Perhaps the shapeshifting overmen were the product of some such evolutionary sequence.

"The machines immediately respond to my presence. This time, I expected it. It matters not at all that it has been ten thousand years or more since my last manifestation; once a society has *true* history, nothing can be lost or forgotten, and machines are exceedingly patient. It would not have mattered to those watching for me had I never embarked upon my third expedition—they would have waited forever, without impatience, without disappointment.

"No flying machine this time. No journey. No confrontation. No locking of curious stares by man and

THE HUNGER AND ECSTASY OF VAMPIRES

overman, victim and vampire, primitive and sophisticate. Had I realised what was happening I would have been frightened and appalled, but the process of possession was invisible and painless. The insectile machines came, saw, associated, did their work and dissolved.

"The touch, when it came, was almost imperceptible.

"What the machines did, essentially, was to make more machines, even tinier than they: ephemeral machines whose magnitude was akin to that of the bacterial organisms which are, as Pasteur has recently proved, the agents of disease. Having done this, they *infected* me with the 'artificial germs' which they had made.

"Were the mechanical germs specifically designed to infect a timeshadow rather than a whole body? If so, how? Does the ability of the machines to employ this mode of communication imply that the overmen have now added this kind of precognition to the repertoire of their mental abilities? *How complete is their mastery of time? Have they, at last, become managers of contingency, architects of destiny?*

"There are, of course, other questions which now have to be added to those which occurred to me as the knowledge of what had been done to me was slowly made clear. Did the infectious agents bind so intimately to my timeshadow that I brought them back with me? *Might they be the seeds of my destruction?*

"That is difficult to believe—far more likely, I think, that only that which I sent forth can possibly return—but perhaps this is mere wishful thinking. In thirty thousand years, what might men not accomplish?

"I mean, of course, not men but *overmen*....if the overmen are to be believed, mere men are too violent to be

THE HUNGER AND ECSTASY OF VAMPIRES

capable of much achievement, too ready to destroy one another and hence to destroy themselves....

"What, in the end, did I actually *do* in the course of my third excursion into the future? Nothing—or nearly nothing. I walked to the top of the hill, where I found a gap in the forest canopy, beneath which green grass grew (left there for my benefit?—surely that is too narcissistic an interpretation?). There, I was able to see the blue sky which I had always known, and the white clouds, and the yellow halo of the sun.

"Later, I was able to see the stars....the same, fixed stars. I was able to see everything that was *constant*, everything which linked my world to the world in which I had come. I was allowed to see that nothing truly fundamental had changed.

"All I actually *did*, with my absurdly heavy-seeming half-body, was to walk to the crest of a hill and sit down on the grass, for half a day and half a night, or perhaps a little more. And yet I saw the world of the overmen, in all its grandeur and glory!

"It was surely not an experience planned and executed solely for my benefit; it was, I must accept, a kind of adventure available to any and every inhabitant of that fabulous era. In that far future, no mind will require the carriage of the body to go wandering, nor will any require the kind of crude separation which my time machine induces. Perhaps the overmen have finally mastered the art of timeshadow projection (far more cleverly than I, if so), but it is more than likely that they have not bothered, because they have something far better. They have machines which can infect a body like the agents of disease, but are designed for creation rather than malaise. They have machines too tiny to see, which breed in the blood and swarm about the brain—yes, even the anaemic fluids which course throughout a timeshadow, even the shadow-brain which a timeshadow has—and which, in time, induce the brightest and most brilliant of fevers: the fever of synthetic experience; the fever of artificial memory; the fever of knowledge.

"I wish I could say 'wisdom' instead of knowledge....and perhaps that was what the machines were designed to give me, had I only had a complete body. Perhaps what they did give me was incomplete and distorted, by virtue of my attenuation. Perhaps, If I had only been whole, the overmen could have filled me with all their wealth of understanding....and perhaps they tried to do exactly that.

"Perhaps, on the other hand, they *do* fear the vicious circle which might result from the communication of too much knowledge from future to present (or present to past). Perhaps they were very careful to give me a vision without coherence....a vivid dream censored of all that might enable me to hasten its actualization.

"There is no way of knowing. What I have is what I have. What I did, within the spaces of my skull, while I sat in the clearing in that alien forest, is what I *did*.....

"I have walked on the surface of the planet Mars: the Mars which we see but dimly through our telescopes; the arid, near-airless Mars of pink sands and jagged ridges, awesome clefts and gouged-out craters; the Mars of my today. And I have walked on the surface of *their* Mars: the Mars of the overmen; the moist, scented Mars of purple skies and blue-black forests; the Mars of seemingly-eternal half-light; the Mars of gargantuan gliders and gossamer-winged skycraft; the Mars of *their* today....

THE HUNGER AND ECSTASY OF VAMPIRES

"I have walked on the surface of Titan, satellite of Saturn: the Titan which is to us a mere point of light; the Titan entombed by many kinds of ice; bare, brutal, lonely Titan. I have walked, too, on the Titan of the overmen: the Titan of crystalline cities; the Titan of domed jungles; lush, lovely, hectic Titan. And from both stations I looked up at Saturn itself; at Saturn's rings; at the gaseous face whose features had, in the second instance, at last begun to change, to harden, to become distinct.....

"I have seen the worlds inside the asteroids: the hollow worlds whose inhabitants had remade themselves, four-armed because they had no need of legs. I had no need to walk there either, and so I flew, on wings which were a part of me, and danced their four-handed jigs all around the decorated walls....

"I have seen the earths which orbit other stars: the myriad earths, the countless Edens. I have trod the streets and soils of worlds where life has followed other paths than ours. I have seen and *known* sentient creatures made in every image and none, some like earthly animals or plants, others seemingly, mineral and some without fixed form at all. I have heard their speech and their music—and I have seen too that these species, like the overmen, obtain in the end command over their own forms, their own attributes, their own ambitions....

"I have seen the wonderful wilderness of life in the sidereal system: the life of a million worlds; the life of a thousand starfaring cultures; the life which fills the great gaseous clouds between the stars; the life which is irrepressible, uncontainable, ever-changing. I have watched the many meetings of the minds and bodies of different species, have been party to their communions, their mergings and their separations....

THE HUNGER AND ECSTASY OF VAMPIRES

"I have not seen mankind. In all of that, *I have not seen mankind.*

"The satyrs and the centaurs passed into oblivion without eventual issue; the descendants of my own kind never found an upward path of progress to follow for a second time. *Homo sapiens* will die, and will be gone for ever; ours is a broken strand upon the loom of destiny, *but it does not matter.* Our kings and queens, our capitalists and merchants, our servants and factory-hands, will give no children to this vast unpatterned confusion, but all that we are and represent—our every thought, our every property—is there.

"In this great scheme, the overmen are our brothers and not our conquerors; they are our other selves, our heirs, our ambassadors to the universe. In this vast overarching scheme, *all* species are our brothers, our other selves. We are life, and life is everywhere, the image of God in which we are made is neither a face nor a form nor even a soul, but a movement, an *impulse*, a *will* to exist, to grow and to change, to be and to become....

"I have seen the worlds which the overmen have come to know, and I have seen that I belong there no less than they....

"Is it an illusion? Is it simply an effect of my infection by the tiny machines which they left to tutor me?

"Perhaps. How can I know? How can I know whether any of it is more than mere illusion, or some feverish effect of this infection which I have unleashed upon myself with my seer's potion, my subtle poison, my loquacious oracle?

"While I lay down on that hillside, I was dreaming. It was *all* a dream, and a dream inside a dream at that....but within the dream within the dream there were further dreams, worlds within worlds.

THE HUNGER AND ECSTASY OF VAMPIRES

"Like a spark of light, and as fleet, I soared among the stars.

"I saw the sidereal system from without, and from its light-filled heart. I saw stars born from dark dust, and I saw stars die, in vast explosions which left behind mere shrinking embers, which collapsed and collapsed and collapsed until nothing was left of them but the purest form of nothing, the ultimate blackness, the shadow of eternity.

"I saw, outside the sidereal system, other such systems, each one surrounded by a cage of darkness so huge and so dense as to beggar the imagination, and I saw these systems extending into unimaginable distances, millions upon millions of them, all flying apart as if they were the debris of an explosion which was the universe itself....

"It is oddly easy, now, to believe that the universe itself is *not* something still, something settled, something made and left for dead, but rather something happening, and happening *violently*, something growing and changing, and that time itself is a headlong rush.....

"We think of ourselves and our world as calm things—nearly tranquil, almost still—*but we are not*. We are universes ourselves, filled with tiny creatures, fevered by their intangible attentions. There is so much darkness in the world without, and in our inner being too, that we think of existence as a faint and flickering thing in a great illimitable void, *but it is not*—for the darkness of the void without and the void within likewise reflect the limitations of our senses, and not the absence of process.

"Within and without, we and the world are far more alive than we know, and it does not matter, in the end, that each and every one of us will die, that the race of men will

THE HUNGER AND ECSTASY OF VAMPIRES

die, that the race of overmen will die, that the universal explosion itself will leave behind nothing in the end but the purest form of nothing, the ultimate blackness—because *everything* is a part of *everything*....

"That is the one and only truth, the one and only destiny.

"Did I truly dream all that, or did I simply *come to know it?* Is it a conclusion reached by my own effort, or something the machines fed into me, already whole, roiling rhetoric and all? Does it *matter*, given that it is there inside me, woven into the fabric of my soul, capable of flowing from pen to page?

"How shall I tell others what I have seen?

"Above all, slowly and gently, one step at a time. Were they to read this without adequate preparation they would simply think me mad. Perhaps I *am* mad. Perhaps the function of the machines which invaded me was to derange me, to destroy me, to make certain that my glimpses of the future could not change the past. But that would probably be unnecessary. Is there any hope at all of alerting men to the presence in their midst of those whose descendants will be the overmen? If they could be alerted, could they do anything to alter their fate? Could they become less warlike, less self-destructive, less blind to their destiny?

"It is a conundrum I cannot hope to solve alone; I must have help.

"I saw....how can I possibly record all that I saw? How can I even remember it? It is fading already in my consciousness, dying like a dream which the waking mind tries with all its might to trap and hold, but loses in the end....and after all, what I did was to lie upon the grass, staring up into the darkening sky, watching the stars come out.

THE HUNGER AND ECSTASY OF VAMPIRES

All else was but an illusion, a disease of the brain, a disturbance in my soul....except, of course, that it was *true*.

"All true, and all real: preserved, synthesized, packaged, projected into the theatre of my mind by some infinitesimal fantasmagoria or kinematograph, but quite real.

"*I have walked upon the surface of the planet Mars, today and tomorrow.* I have seen the planet dead and I have seen it brought to life.

"I have seen tomorrow's creators labouring in their laboratories to make and reshape life. I have seen the hustle and bustle of Creation: not the work of a mock-fatherly God overfond of prohibitions and petty acts of vengeance, but the work of men who are able to manipulate germ-plasm, who have mastery of the mysteries of the flesh. I have not seen the maker of stars crying *fiat lux* into the darkness, but I have seen the makers of overmen and the remakers of worlds, busy in the crucible from which all the Golden Ages of the future will be born.

"I have come face to face with the black eyes of the infinite, and met their terrifying stare—not bravely enough, I admit, but not so steeped in terror as to be struck blind...or dumb...or dead.

"It was not all seeing and hearing, of course. The things which infected my brain, to bring the news of infinity and eternity directly to my synapses were masters of all the senses, and all the emotions. I felt the texture of the future, the rhythm of the spheres, in the secret chambers of my heart....

"What nonsense! Am I not a man of science, a man of precision? What respect will anyone have for me if I descend to such fatuous nonsense? And yet....the machines which undertook the task of my education did try to make me feel what no human could ever feel for himself; they did try to communicate to me

THE HUNGER AND ECSTASY OF VAMPIRES

what the existence of an overman is like, from the standpoint of an overman's self-regard.

"What little did I salvage from that, and how can I possibly describe it?

"How, indeed?

"Very well....*I have looked at the world with an overman's eyes.* I have responded as he would respond. I have stood in the shoes of an overman of my own day, of my own present, and have looked at my fellow men with his eyes, with his fearful and resentful heart, with his *hunger.*

"Oh yes, I have felt the hunger of vampires....the hunger and ecstasy of vampires.

"I am the prey, privileged to have felt the anticipatory surge of the predator's blood; I am the unwary, privileged to have felt the uncalm consciousness of the hidden; I am the human, privileged to have felt the triumph of the superhuman.

"I have tasted and *understood* the hunger and ecstasy of vampires. I have seen the altar on which mankind is to be sacrificed—and I have worshipped at that altar.

"I have stood in the shoes of an overman of the far future, too. I have known what it is to have tamed hunger and ecstasy, to have brought them to heel, to have made them docile.

"*They wanted me to stay!* That which possessed me begged me to stay and not return, begged me to consent....but I could not. I could not do it. I dared not do it. My sense of duty was stronger, in the end, than their temptation.

"Perhaps I *am* mad.

THE HUNGER AND ECSTASY OF VAMPIRES

"I have known the peace of the ultimate overmen, and would not accept it as a gift. I have been in Heaven, and threw myself out, like a sinful angel, to fall through all eternity into the blackness of the pit.

"Yes, I am mad...but I have known *ataraxia*, the perfect peace of mind—which comes not from the strangulation of emotion, not from the transcendence of the passions, not from mechanization or denial or anaesthesia but from *discipline*, from *control*...and I have understood what it was in men that had to die, lest mankind itself should die....and, of course, *did* die....to be replaced by something gentler, kinder, wiser, *better*....something which emerged from the dark edges of nightmares, from the anxious recesses of myth, to be—when seen in its own light—something merely *different*, and not so very different at that: a blurred mirror-image, but recognisably akin. A brother.

"A *blood*-brother.

"If only we could recognise what we truly are, we would surely be less afraid of what we are not.

"If only we could see the monster which we are making of ourselves, we might be able to see that which is less than monstrous in the images of fear and hate which our minds conjure up so vividly and so prolifically....

"I might have stayed, but I could not. I might have stayed, but I did not. I chose to return, to my poor poisoned self, my poor dying body, my time of tragedy.

"If only....

"I am ill. There is no doubt about it. Not because I have carried back any vestige of that glorious delirium with which the machines of the far future infected me so carefully....they are gone; I cannot doubt it. I am ill because of what I have done to myself.

"The good doctor was right about the dangers, the convulsions. I am poisoned. In seeking to gain intelligence of the future I have cut myself adrift from the present. Did the seers of old understand that there was a price to pay for overmuch success? Did the sibyls who served the ancients fully understand their self-sacrifice?

"Why did I not stay? Why did I not accept the gift that was offered?

"God how my arm aches! What a rack my grip upon the pen has become!

"I ought to write all day and all night. I ought to write and write, until I have wrung from my inarticulate heart every last vestige of the knowledge by which I have been possessed....but I cannot. Forgive me, but I *cannot*.

"If I am to tell my story at all I must tell it verbally, *all* of it—tell it in a single night, if I can, to men that I can trust....men who might understand. If only I knew a hundred who might *begin* to understand....

"If only I knew ten.

"If only....."

* * * *

20

The doctor looked up from the manuscript. He had been reading like an automaton, but with evident effort.

"I fear," he said, uneasily, "that Copplestone had reached the limit of his endurance, and the limit of his legibility. He did try to continue, but there are only a few more words I can decipher. He tried, at least, to make a list of some kind....perhaps a list of topics accessory to what I have just read, which were to be added to a later draft. I will read those which I can make out. To the best of my estimation, the list includes the following:

"*Hist Reconst. Great War. Wire and Gas. Vampires don't kill. Hide in Comfort. Atom Bomb. Birth Pills. Silicon Clips. Vs love flying. Thrive in cities—art light. Land on moor. Great Plague War. Oceans die, then rise. Ozone shield. Shapeshifters immune to rad poison. Proofs. Electricity. Cathode rays.* There are half a dozen other items of which I can make no sense at all.

"At the foot of the last page, separate from the rest of the text, a list of five surnames has been scribbled. Mine is one—the only one not followed by a question-mark. Sir William Crookes is another; Wilde's and Shiel's are there also. The last is, I think, Stoker."

THE HUNGER AND ECSTASY OF VAMPIRES

My overloaded train of thought was jolted very slightly by that name, but there was far too much to wonder at without bothering with such an insignificant reflex.

What a reward I have reaped by following my instinct! I thought. *What a wise providence it was which led me to steal the elixir and the secret of its making! How could I ever have doubted my impulse or my destiny, even for a moment? Everything is clear now, everything settled, everything right. All my life—all my wicked, wretched, wilful life—has been naught but an enigmatic prologue, a prelude to this moment. How can I doubt it? Even before I heard the summons loud and clear, I did what I had to do. All my life I have been groping towards the kindly light, hardly knowing how blind I was. And now, it is clear. At last, it is clear.*

Even Wilde, I knew, could not possibly complain about a lack of imaginative excess in the peculiar diatribe which we had just heard...but even a man like Wilde might struggle in vain to penetrate the meaning of the bolder half of it. Infectious machines! A universe of teeming vermin! Existence as explosion! The ultimate nothing! Was even he, I wondered, capable of seeing it as something more than a mere fever-dream, not far removed from gibberish? Was Crookes—or Shiel—or the imaginatively ambitious Wells? I was all agog to find out.

As for myself, I had no doubts at all. If Copplestone had not seen the future, I was certain that he had certainly seen something: something that no man of this or any earlier time had ever seen before.

Let it be the future! I said to myself, silently. *Great Father of us All, let it be the future of destiny, unalterable by any human deed or freak of chance!*

THE HUNGER AND ECSTASY OF VAMPIRES

"No doubt that Copplestone would have give us a much clearer account of his final adventure had he been able to do so," said the doctor, awkwardly. Clearly he had had only the vaguest notion of what the manuscript contained before he began to read, and now had not the slightest notion of what it all signified. "No doubt he would have prepared us far better to discuss its implications...."

"I am not sure that any elaborate discussion is necessary," his friend put in. "We have all heard the story—or as much of it as Copplestone contrived to reveal—and each one of us will doubtless make of it what he will. There are other matters which require our immediate consideration."

"On the contrary," Wilde said. "We are here at Copplestone's invitation, for a purpose which he defined. He has gone to some trouble to make his story known to us, and our first duty is surely to do what he required of us: to make our reactions known to one another, and exchange views as to the precise implications of what he had seen. We have accepted the man's hospitality, and we owe him that, even though he is not here to listen to us?"

The Great Detective threw up his hands. "Oh, very well!" he said. "There is time to waste, I suppose. Justice is rarely swift, but it is inexorable." He looked at me as he pronounced this blatant lie, but I looked calmly back.

"Perhaps," said Wilde, effortlessly usurping the doctor's role as chairman, "Mr. Wells would like to begin, as he has been enthusiastic to point out certain similarities between Copplestone's vision of the future and his own."

The young man was shier now than he had been, and the proffered opportunity was not entirely welcome. Nevertheless, he took it up. "I freely admit," he said, slowly, "that the similarities are, in the end, less striking than the differences. Nevertheless, the similarities are still a matter of some interest to me. I will accept that no conscious imitation can have been involved, and that unconscious imitation is unlikely—although the possibility remains, I think, that someone who read the first version of my story in the *Science Schools Journal* might in the course of the last few years have communicated its contents to Professor Copplestone in such a manner that he built a fantasy of his own upon their foundation.

"I regret, however, that I cannot seriously entertain Sir William's hypothesis that I am a true seer who has glimpsed—as through a glass, darkly—the same future which Copplestone has seen in more detail. I would rather fall back on the less dramatic but more likely hypothesis that Copplestone and I are both products of our milieu and our moment. We shared the same present day for some thirty years, and probably acquired much the same understanding of it. Although he was older than I and born into a different class he must have undergone broadly similar educative experiences. He found Darwin's theory of evolution, as I did, and realised with a shock as profound as any religious enlightenment what it implies about the precariousness of man's tenure upon the earth. He came to appreciate, as I have, that the rapid advancement of technology will very soon equip our armies with weapons so powerful that we might easily destroy civilization before learning to curb our primitive impulses. If he and I have visited the Delphic Oracle of the modern imagination and come back with similar prophesies, it is because the Age of Reason has now reached the stage at which secure *rational* foresight is possible."

THE HUNGER AND ECSTASY OF VAMPIRES

He paused for thought, but soon continued. "There is, of course, much in Copplestone's vision which is purely idiosyncratic. He knew this too, and freely admitted the probability that his vision would be polluted, in the way that all our dreams are polluted, by random imps of perversity. In each and every one of us there is a constant battle being fought between a higher, rational part and a lower, animal part. Copplestone's vision is clearly haunted by a strange darkness which persists in populating his imagined future with phantoms–the phantoms which he calls vampires. I do not think that we should take Copplestone's vampires any more literally than we take Polidori's *Vampyre*, or Christina Rossetti's goblins. They are, I think, *symbols*: symbols of something which lies within us, but which we feel, in concert with the prudery of our times, that we ought to exorcise or deny.

"I believe that Copplestone protests far too much when he insists that his overmen are not men at all, but some other species which has lived since the dawn of time among men, mimicking them in order to prey upon them. I think that we should look for the source of Copplestone's imaginary vampires in the blood which is supposedly their nourishment: the blood which carries the chemical messengers which are the bases of our feelings, our desires and our passions. It is clear, I think, from the tenor of the professor's narrative–especially in the final part, which is surely the product of a purely subjective delirium–that he could not quite escape the essential truth. Despite all his attempts to distance himself, he ended up identifying with the vampires, seeing as they saw and feeling as they felt. What he saw in that final vision is far more closely related to his private mental life than to any meaningful picture of what the future could or will be like.

The heavy emphasis on the idea of infection proves that, to my mind, beyond the shadow of a doubt.

"In brief, I think that there may be a little truth in the earlier phases of Copplestone's story, but I cannot believe that it arrived there by any occult means, and I do not think that the story has any real relevance to the question of whether the future which will come to be is already destined, or merely contingent on decisions and discoveries we might or might not make."

It was an impressive speech, in its way, and I was glad to hear it. I suspected that it would set a sober and sententious tone for what would follow, and might well draw the entire discussion into a blind alley. I had not the slightest objection to such a deflection.

"Thank you," said the doctor. "Mr. Shiel, would you like to comment on what your friend has said?"

The curly-haired man hesitated before replying. His experience, I think, had been a little closer to mine than to his friend's. He had felt the same shock, the same thrill....but he was *young*, and did not yet know how to trust the wisdom of his soul.

"It might easily take half a lifetime," he said, eventually, "fully to digest the implications of what we have heard these last two nights. In broad terms, Wells is probably right. We cannot doubt that Copplestone really experienced these things, and we must be prepared to consider, if only as an hypothesis, that there is *some* truth in his vision. It does seem probable that the vampires of his dream are not what Copplestone took them to be....but I wonder whether it might not be the case that the final vision was the *most* rather than the *least* truthful: the one least confused by the impish froth

THE HUNGER AND ECSTASY OF VAMPIRES

of pure dream. I wonder whether that incredibly hectic and vivid vision might not have been the grasping of the very essence of evolutionary process and universal destiny...."

He was warming to his task now. "If there is a lesson to be learned from this dream," he went on, "it is a lesson in the politics of evolution, and the irresistibility of progress. If there is a revelation in it—and I am prepared to entertain the notion that the mind of God is occasionally reflected in the tinier thoughts of man—it is a revelation which speaks to us of the way in which life is forever destined to *climb* towards dizzy heights of enlightenment.

"The arrogance which informed men that they were at the centre of creation, that the earth and the universe entire had been made for them, is something which must now be put away with other childish things; we must realise and understand that there will indeed be *overmen* whose task it will be to take up the torch of progress when our imperfections lead us to exhaustion. We should not see this supersession as a terrible thing, but as a confirmation of the fact that our sojourn upon this earth has not been in vain, and that the gift of our blood—which is surely symbolic of the heritage which we shall pass on to our successors—is well worth the giving. The fact that our species is, indeed, doomed to disappear should delight us rather than disappointing us, once we understand that we are to give way to another which is better and bolder, which will build so magnificently on foundations that we have laid as to become godlike in ambition and achievement.

"If what we have heard is a dream and only a dream, then I will say this: men who can dream such dreams are already overmen in embryo. To the extent that the future is not predestined it must be built out of the dreams of the present; if men were not capable of dreaming such dreams as this they would be unable to produce futures of any kind akin to that previsioned here, and that would be a tragedy.

"Let us not worry unduly as to the exact truth or falsehood of this particular vision; let us be profoundly glad that a man has proved himself capable of dreaming thus, and let us hope that we ourselves might not be incapable of similar triumphs."

I saw one or two of the others—including Wilde—smile indulgently at Shiel's wild enthusiasm, but the doctor's friend was the only one whose eyes were raised impatiently to heaven.

It was Crookes who took up the thread.

"I am naturally disappointed," he said, gravely, "that the insights into the nature and possible applications of electricity which Copplestone hoped to offer us have not in the end materialized. But I have more than one field of scientific interest, and Copplestone's adventure bears on the other as well. We are on the threshold of a new era of discovery in the science of apparitions and communication with the spirits of the dead, and it seems to me that what Copplestone has achieved is yet another proof of the reality of apparitions.

"If this story is to be taken seriously—and like these young men, I cannot doubt its sincerity, although I certainly doubt that its conclusion was any more than a delirious episode—then the intriguing possibility is raised that at least some apparitions may be what Copplestone calls *timeshadows* rather than shades of the departed, and it may well be that some of the confusion which presently arises in the course of communication with what are assumed to be spirits is

THE HUNGER AND ECSTASY OF VAMPIRES

accountable in these terms. I would certainly like to bring Copplestone's story to the attention of my colleagues in the Society for Psychical Research....and I think some of them may be better qualified than I to speculate about the possible reality of vampires. Tesla, of course, will not agree with me...."

This was an unwise inclusion in what might have been a much longer discourse. Tesla, as Sir William had anticipated, did not agree, and wanted to make his disagreement clear.

"It'd take more than a few suggestions about the nature of ghosts to recompense *me* for the loss of Copplestone's supposed discoveries in electrical science," the American said. "And when a promise like that is made and not fulfilled, an American begins to smell hokum. I know this guy is a professor, and I know all about your English regard for the word of a gentleman, but can we at least take seriously the possibility that this whole thing is a straightforward hoax, or at best a tissue of fantasies generated by monomania?

"It seems to me that Copplestone exaggerated his understanding of Darwin's theory of evolution if he couldn't see that any ability to see the future, drug-assisted or not, would be so advantageous to any critter that had it that it'd be selected out in no time at all—and yet we're supposed to accept that men, who do have it, will get replaced by vampires, who don't. I guess he intended to get around that with the help of this shilly-shallying about the future of destiny and the future of contingency, on the grounds that the prophetic gift would only be useful if it actually allowed us to *change* things, but I don't buy that. I think we've been taken for a ride here. I don't know why, but I think we've been fed a pack of lies, just like Mr. Wilde here has said."

THE HUNGER AND ECSTASY OF VAMPIRES

"I fear," said Wilde, "that my earlier comments may have been open to misinterpretation. When I referred to Copplestone's story as a lie, the word was not intended as an insult. Quite the contrary—the modern world's dedication to vulgar truth is something I deeply regret, not because I have anything against the truth, but because the modern notion of what truth is has become so very narrow. The modern obsession with petty facts and meaningless measurements distresses me almost as much as the triviality of modern mendacity—for I would never dignify the banal deceptions of politicians and advertising men by calling them *lies*.

"Lies, to my mind, are grandiose products of the imagination, which enlarge the truth rather than diminishing it. When I describe Copplestone's experience as a lie I only mean to imply what he attempted to convey by speaking of it as a vision or a hallucination, admitting its inevitable pollution by the hopes and fears hidden in the recesses of his inmost soul. Even if it had been a lie in the sense of being a manifest fiction—like the story which Mr. Wells has described to us—I would not say that it could not, therefore, function as a veritable fount of wisdom. Any man who did say such a thing would be a fool, and I am sure that Mr. Wells will agree with me on that point. Let us not occupy ourselves with the vulgar matter of whether Copplestone's account is false in any trivial sense— rather let us concentrate on what it has to teach us because and in spite of the fact that it is a lie of unparalleled boldness and magnificence."

Tesla was clearly unconvinced, and the grey-eyed man's expression was openly contemptuous. Wilde, of course, continued regardless. "What Copplestone tells us, in brief, is that the universe in which we live is a more wonderful place than our half-blind senses and meagre minds can easily perceive or imagine. That is surely true—or, at any rate, we ought to hope fervently that it might be. He informs us, too, that we should not be overly vain about the accomplishments of mankind, which might easily evaporate in a reckless moment in order that we may give way to a better species, the fact of whose supersession would naturally embody both our most intimate fears and our most daring ambitions. That too is true—or, again, we should certainly hope so. Perhaps most importantly of all, Copplestone tells us that we are capable, each and every one of us, of adventures of the mind far bolder than any we have so far dared to undertake, and that however dangerous or confusing such adventures may turn out to be, the brave man will not shirk them. Can anyone, even for a moment, doubt the truth of *that*—or doubt, at any rate, that they ought to wish with all their hearts that it *might* be true?"

I looked around. There seemed to be some who did doubt it.

"I could not have put it better, Oscar," I said, drily. I did my best to sound flippant and ironic." Indeed, *no one* could have put it better. There is not a word to add."

Even Wilde—whose appetite for flattery was insatiable—frowned a little, as if to say that he had meant what he said more seriously than my casual endorsement implied.

The Great Detective was still impatient to turn the discussion towards matters of his own concern. "I have a keener appetite than Mr. Wilde for the separation of the improbable from the impossible," he said. "For myself, I am less interested in the possibility that Copplestone's story may contain hints about the actual shape of the far future than the probability that it contained clues as to a motive for robbery. We know that Copplestone intended to offer all of us the opportunity of using his drug to put his story to the proof—and we know that someone has taken the trouble to reserve that privilege entirely to himself. I cannot help wondering why—what motive could possibly have impelled someone seated here to do such a thing? If Sir William or Mr. Tesla really believed that the drug might disclose new insights in electrical science one of them might have thought it worth while monopolising the advantage—but they have not been given adequate grounds for believing that. If Mr. Wells or Mr. Shiel felt that the drug might be an invaluable aid to the furtherance of their budding literary careers, they might have thought it worthwhile to take possession of the formula— but they are young men, and I think they have confidence enough in their own powers of invention. Mr. Wilde is not so young, but he has the confidence of ten men in his ability to lie effectively."

"Whereas I," I put in, smoothly, "have no conceivable motive at all. It is clear, therefore, that Mr. Wells was right about where the theft took place. It must have been you who picked your friend's pocket after he had taken off his jacket, and you who removed the vial while you friend was busy with Copplestone's corpse. It only remains for you to tell us why on earth you did it!"

There was a ripple of laughter, not so much because what I had said was hilarious, but because everyone was embarrassed by the man's dogged insistence that a crime had been committed and that someone seated at the table must therefore be a blackguard. The detective's scowl deepened, but he must have known that had he charged me with the theft the laughter would have increased.

Even so, I was grateful that we were at that moment interrupted, when Copplestone's manservant brought in a message which had been delivered to the door. He gave the message to the doctor.

"It is from the doctors at King's who conducted the *post mortem* examination," the physician said, when he had scanned it. "They attribute Copplestone's death to the general deterioration of his vital organs caused by his use, over a long period, of certain poisonous compounds. There was no evidence of any ingestion of poison within the last twenty-four hours. There is a separate note to the effect that in the absence of any evidence of breaking and entering, Scotland Yard will not be mounting an investigation of the missing vial. The matter is officially closed...."

He trailed off, leaving something unsaid.

"It may be officially closed," said his friend, darkly, "but it is not ended."

It was Sir William who took it upon himself to prompt the doctor, although I too had guessed what it was that had perplexed him.

"How great was the deficit?" asked the man of science.

The doctor looked up, clearly embarrassed. "What deficit?" he said, although he knew very well.

"Come now," said Crookes. "The doctors at King's may not have considered the matter significant—after all, the weight of a body is a simple datum, if you have nothing with which to compare it—but *you* have been weighing Copplestone before and after his experiments for some little while. *How much weight had Copplestone's corpse lost?*"

"About three stones," said the doctor. "It seemed very light when I examined it, of course, but...."

"Death is not the end," Sir William said, triumphantly, as if he were quoting the final line of a mathematical proof. "This we know."

THE HUNGER AND ECSTASY OF VAMPIRES

"But he did not take the contents of the vial," the doctor said. "The *post mortem* confirms that."

"Perhaps," said Crookes, "he no longer needed the drug. Perhaps the drug merely helped him to teach himself the art of astral projection."

"You aren't saying, I hope, that he might yet *come back?*" said Tesla.

Crookes shook his grizzled head. "He said once that the body which a timeshadow left behind would probably not survive any mortal damage to the timeshadow—but it is possible, is it not, that a timeshadow might survive the death of the body? It is, I think, very probable that some such phantom always does. Is it possible, do you think, that whatever Copplestone encountered in the farther reaches of his expedition, could reach back to his point of origin, not to destroy but to *save* him? Perhaps, in the end, Copplestone overcame his fear of attack, and found himself able to accept the invitation which the world into which he went—which may well have been something other than the far future—made to him. Perhaps, in the end, he could not resist the temptation."

"This is madness," said Tesla. Crookes did not take offence—it was he, after all, who had invited Tesla to accompany him—but simply shrugged his shoulders.

"This exchange of views does not seem to be getting us anywhere," said the grey-eyed man, acidly.

"Perhaps you are right," said Wilde. "Perhaps we expect too much of reasoned discussion—or of our own ability to make use of it. We are only human, after all. Each of us is locked within his own theories, imprisoned by his own prejudices....and there can be no proof of anything that we have heard. Even if we still had the drug, and one of us the courage to use it, there would be no proof. It is, and must remain, a lie: a rough-hewn, but nevertheless brilliant, lie. Even if we undertook to believe it, it would become a lie again as soon as we tried to persuade anyone else of its truth. Professor Copplestone might have done well to remember the story of Cassandra—the wise parable which reminds us that prophets, no matter how accurate they may be, can *never* command belief."

He looked around to make sure that everyone appreciated the point he was making, and I looked around with him.

They do not care! I thought, as I studied the expressions on their faces. *They are prepared to be serious about it, and to play at philosophy, but they do not care. It is too remote from their ordinary lives. Wells, Shiel and Wilde are as forward-looking as any men in the world, but even they regard this as an intellectual game. They can see no relevance to themselves—and that is why it has no relevance to themselves. I alone had the vision to steal the vial. I alone had the intelligence to steal the formula. The future is mine, and mine alone, because I was the only one among them who cared enough to steal it.*

"Very well," Wilde concluded. "We must be content with what we have, and each and every one of us must make of it what he can. Now, sir, do you have some specific charge to bring against one of us, or will you let us go to our homes?"

"I have no charge to bring, *at present*," said the master of ratiocination, "but you may be sure that the matter of the formula and the vial will not be forgotten."

I offered the detective and the doctor a lift in my carriage, but the detective declined. I was not overly surprised.

THE HUNGER AND ECSTASY OF VAMPIRES

I suspected that I had not seen the last of him, and that the next time we met, it would not be as friends.

* * * *

21

The inevitable came to pass a little more than seventy-two hours later, when I returned to the house which I had rented in a quiet cul-de-sac off the Edgware Road in the early hours. The Great Detective must have lain in wait, watching the house, for some considerable time. He did not show himself immediately, but waited until the carriage had been driven round into the mews. As I set down my burden in order to bring out my keys he called my name from the bottom of the flight of steps which led up to the front door. I turned to confront him.

"How pleasant to see you again," I murmured.

"The pleasure is mutual," he assured me, with even greater insincerity. "I am sorry to come calling at such an hour—had I been able to find you earlier in the day I would have done so. May I help you with your case?"

"No thank you," I said. "It is not heavy, and its contents are delicate. I would rather have charge of it myself."

"I presume that it contains the last of the ingredients required to make up Copplestone's formula," he said, carefully maintaining the same conversational tone.

I smiled—a little wanly, no doubt. I pushed the door open before turning to meet his gaze again.

THE HUNGER AND ECSTASY OF VAMPIRES

"Would you like to come in?" I asked.

"I would."

"In that case," I said, standing away from the open door, "Please do. Enter freely, of your own will, I beg of you."

When our coats and hats were hung up in the hallway I conducted him into the sitting-room. The fire had burned very low, there being no servants in the house to maintain it, but when I had lit the candles I added more wood, and stirred it with the poker until the embers flared. I offered my visitor the armchair to the right of the hearth, but before lowering myself into the one to the left I went to the sideboard where there was a decanter of whisky.

"Would you like a drink?" I asked. "I have no liking for alcohol myself, but I keep a little for my guests."

"I think not," he said. There was an edge to his voice now. Apparently he suspected that I might poison him, although my only desire was to help him to relax. Lest that should prove impossible—I did not know how seriously to take his reputation as a man with a preternaturally sharp mind—I opened the right-hand drawer of the sideboard, shielding the action with my body. I took out the gun which rested there—but when I turned with it in my hand, I saw that the detective had a gun of his own. He was touching his chin lightly with the barrel.

"I fear," I said, with a theatrical sigh, "that we have reached an *impasse*."

"Hardly," he said. "What you have there is an antique duelling pistol, which can only fire one shot even if it happens to be loaded. What I have here is the doctor's old army revolver, which is a more accurate weapon by far and is fully loaded with six bullets. I think I have the advantage, don't you?"

"Can you be fully confident of the efficacy of *any* gun?" I asked him, mockingly. "Have you spoken to Arminius Vambery about me?"

"The professor is in Budapest," my adversary replied, "But I spoke to someone who was at the Beefsteak Club five years ago, when Vambery entertained the party with bloodcurdling tales of the vampires of Eastern Europe."

"Then you must know that garlic and a crucifix are better tools than a pistol to keep a *vampire* at bay. Have you doused yourself in holy water? Have you a sharpened wooden stake about you, perchance? We have quite a while to wait until dawn, I fear. I suppose you will be anxious at least until you see that I will not vanish away, nor shrivel to dust beneath the rays of the sun."

"You never go out by day," he said, off-handedly. "That much I have ascertained for sure."

I sat down, not more than eight feet away from him. I did not point my gun at him, nor did he point his at me, but neither one of us laid his weapon down. I knew that it would be some time before he relaxed sufficiently to be mesmerized, but the hour was late and his chair was comfortable.

"My skin and eyes are extraordinarily sensitive to sunlight," I told him. "London's grey pall is far less of a menace than the bluer skies of Italy or Greece, but my habits were formed in brighter climes and London's night-life is so much more interesting than its daylit routines."

He looked at the candles on the mantelpiece, and at the unlit gas-light on the wall. "Even indoors," he observed, "you seem to like gentle light. Would you prefer it, perhaps, if the candle-flames burned bluer?"

I laughed. "You seem confused as to which kind of vampire I might be," I observed.

THE HUNGER AND ECSTASY OF VAMPIRES

"There is no such thing as a vampire," he informed me. "There are no undead stalking the streets for prey, and there are no mimics skulking in the hills waiting for mankind to destroy itself. I am not a superstitious man, Count Lugard. Still, it would be interesting to hear *your* version of Arminius Vambery's slanderous story—and an explanation of your reasons for stealing Copplestone's formula from the doctor's coat when you collided with him as he was trying to board your carriage."

"Where *is* the good doctor?" I asked. "According to his accounts of your adventures you rarely go anywhere without him—except, of course, to that sanatorium in Switzerland to which you retired a little while ago for a rest cure. How are your nerves now? Have you managed to overcome your addiction to the new opium?"

"Copplestone's manservant eventually confessed his misdemeanour," the Great Detective said, blithely ignoring the fact that we seemed to be talking at cross-purposes. "I know that the girl was in the house, and I know that she had the opportunity to take the vial. She had no motive, of course— she was naught but a common whore—but she was simply executing a commission. She was seen talking to a person of your description—and she has *not* been seen in Piccadilly for three days. The other ladies of the night thought that odd, given that she had stuck so religiously to her pitch for some weeks previously, regardless of the winter cold. On the lookout for someone, they said. Someone special. Not the usual kind of customer."

"What do you suppose I have done with her?" I asked, lightly. "Do you think she scratches even now at the lid of her coffin, desperate to escape in order that she might slake her hunger for human blood?"

THE HUNGER AND ECSTASY OF VAMPIRES

"What *have* you done with her, *Monsieur le Comte?*"
He spoke the phrase as if it were the deadliest of insults, at
last abandoning his show of scrupulous politeness.

"Much as I did with Arminius Vambery's daughter," I
murmured, tiring of the game. "No more—and certainly no
less. "I can tell you where to find her, if you really want to. But
she will not tell you anything about the vial. She would not
even if she could."

"But you *do* have the vial," he said, "do you not?"

"Arminius Vambery is quite mad," I said, quietly. "You
must have realised that, even if your informant did not stress
the fact. Not in every respect, of course. On all subjects but
one he plays the *savant* to perfection, and without
dissimulation....but on that one subject he is the victim of a
terrible delusion. If only he were not so anxious to talk about
it to anyone and everyone, but that is the form and fabric of
his madness. The preposterousness of the story does not
detract from its fascination as a tale, more's the pity. As Oscar
Wilde would doubtless observe, a vivid lie is so much more
memorable than a dull and naked truth."

"It is the dull and naked truth," he assured me, "that I
have come here tonight to ascertain."

I was not overly grateful for that. It might have been
easier, in a way, had he come fully prepared to hear wild
fantasies.

"Very well," I said. "I will tell you the dull and naked
truth. I debauched Vambery's youngest daughter. I did not
bother to persuade myself that I had fallen in love with her; I
did not propose marriage to her. I used her as I had used others.
It was heartless, perhaps cruel. I was a villain. I say nothing in
my defence, not even that I was educated in a hard school.

THE HUNGER AND ECSTASY OF VAMPIRES

I have always been a villain, by instinct and by inclination. None of that matters. The naked truth is that I seduced the girl, in a spirit which had naught to do with love. I learned, later, to regret it—to regret it very bitterly—but I claim no credit for that; I know that it cannot excuse me.

"Vambery swore revenge, and would have tried to take it in an altogether ordinary way, had he any competence with sword or pistol, but he had not. He had naught but the mind and sinews of a professor of languages, and the capacity for obsession which academic study requires and rewards. The seduction of his daughter drove him half-mad, her suicide completed the process. He could not fight me, or murder me, so his burgeoning obsession found other ways to strike out at me. I have regretted ever since that he was not a bigger, braver man. I would far rather he had aimed a bullet at my heart than do to me what he has done these last ten years.

"The dull and naked truth is that my name really is Lugard; the notion that I obtained it by reversing the name Dragul is Vambery's fantasy, as is the absurd proposition that I am some kind of reincarnation or resurrection of the voivode Vlad Dragul, called Tepes or the Impaler, whose name is usually Latinised as Dracul and sometimes rendered Dracula—that is, 'son of Dracul'—in order to distinguish him from his like-named father. It is also Vambery's fantasy that I am one of the undead, who subsists by drinking human blood, and that what I did to his daughter was utterly unnatural and accomplished by magic. The dull and naked truth is that what I did to his daughter was entirely natural, even if a little of the mesmerist's art was employed in its accomplishment. They do say, do they not, that no one can be persuaded even by mesmerism to do anything which flatly contradicts her own will? The Professor, alas, was quite unable to accept that, and felt compelled to invent an alternative account which absolved his beloved child from *all* hint of blame.

"As the late Professor Copplestone scrupulously pointed out to us, a man's vision is ever apt to be polluted, perverted and confused by his hopes, fears and fancies—and Vambery made himself vulnerable to fears and fancies of the worst kind. He has pursued me throughout Europe with dark rumours and direct slanders. He has done his best to ruin my reputation, and to make a demon of me in the eyes of my fellow men. No one believes him, of course—not *literally*—but the lie is so very gaudy, so very *entertaining* that it is repeated anyway. No one really believes that I am Dragul reincarnate, nor that I am an actual vampire which feeds on the blood of my fellow men...but that does not prevent the whispers and the sly glances, and the universal acceptance of the notion that however I accomplished the feat, I did worse than murder Laura Vambery. Vambery has succeeded, after a fashion, in making a vampire of me in the eyes of my fellow men. His caustic lies have stripped me by degrees of every vestige of that respect that was my rightful due by virtue of birth, wealth and station.

"If Wilde's friend Stoker really is writing a book based in the supposed occult wisdom of Arminius Vambery, I shudder to think what a further shadow it might cast upon my life. You ought to sympathise with that, as one who has some experience of the way in which a real life may be confused by myths. If it is difficult to live up to a heroic reputation, think how much more difficult it might be to live down a monstrous one!"

He would not respond to that, but he was sitting less rigidly now. As his curiosity was fed, he was possessed by a soothing tranquillity. What a strange being he was!

THE HUNGER AND ECSTASY OF VAMPIRES

"In a way," I told him, lowering my voice almost to a whisper, "I wish I *were* a vampire. It would almost be better if everything that Vambery has said about me were true. Then, I could not be hurt by his lies—and Laura Vambery could have risen from the grave to become my kin, my consort. Failing that, I would far rather be the kind of being which Copplestone described than a *human* being. In my inmost heart, I wish that every word which Copplestone spoke might be true—that all humanity might be doomed and damned, so that *vampires* might inherit the earth, and worry no more about the stupid hatreds of blind, mad men. Alas, I fear that Copplestone may have been no less a victim of his fears and fancies than Arminius Vambery. The dull truth and the dull tragedy is that you are absolutely right: *there is no such thing as a vampire*."

"Then why," he said, with what was clearly intended as devastating simplicity, "did you steal the professor's formula, and the remainder of his drug? Do you hope to make money selling it, perhaps?"

He was being so lumpenly ironic, and seemed so stubbornly blind to the import of what I had been telling him, that I almost said "Yes"—but it might have jolted him out of his quiet mood.

"You know better than that," I purred. "Do you think my life of leisure is sustained by dealing in opium and absinthe? My wealth is all inherited, and needs no such supplementation. It was my villain's instinct which made me steal the vial and the paper; once having concluded that I wanted them, it was the most natural thing in the world for me to take them. For a little while, I considered the possibility that the impulse was not entirely my own—that it might have been planted in my soul by one of Copplestone's overmen, reaching back through time to make sure that the secret would not die with him—but that is mere romance, is it not? You and I know better than to traffic in such nonsense."

I knew that I was on safe ground. Was this not a man whose watchword was *When you have eliminated the impossible, whatever remains, however implausible, must be the truth*? In pedantic fact, of course, that was the watchword of the doctor's literary invention, and I knew by the haunted expression in his eyes that *this* man was trying desperately to live up to his legend. I, on the other hand, knew perfectly well that if, when you have eliminated the apparently impossible, you are left with something unworthy of consideration, then you might as well start re-examining your assumptions regarding the limits of possibility.

"So you took the vial, although you already had the formula, out of simple dog-in-the-manger selfishness?" he said.

"But of course," I said, gently. The man had little understanding of the true wellsprings of human action; he could not have begun to understand the true complexity of my motives, because they could not have met his crude standards of rationality. He could not have begun to comprehend what the combination of Arminius Vambery's malicious madness and the belated love for Laura Vambery which I had belatedly discovered in my desolate heart had made of me. He was certainly not incapable of obsession himself, but he did not have imagination enough to see where obsession might lead a man with a soul as dark as mine.

Oscar Wilde might have understood, but Wilde was about to set sail on the morrow, headed for the desert sun with his handsome Judas, leaving me alone and friendless.

THE HUNGER AND ECSTASY OF VAMPIRES

"I must ask you to return the formula," said my would-be Nemesis, formally. "You may keep the vial, I suppose, but the formula was consigned to the care of Copplestone's personal physician, and certainly is his by right."

"The written formula no longer exists," I said, regretfully. "I have destroyed the paper I took from the doctor's jacket. It is safe in my memory, but there it will remain."

"I can't believe that," he said—but he said it mechanically, like an automaton. He was mine, now, and I could play him as I wished.

I leaned forward. "You might yet be surprised," I said, "by your own capacity for belief."

"What do you mean by that?" he asked, uneasily. For the first time, the barrel of his gun was directed at my heart, but there was not the slightest possibility that he would fire.

"You ought not to despise this weapon," I said, softly. "I have killed one man with it."

"It was a ricochet which killed Mourier," he said, proudly displaying the extent of the enquiries he had made. "You aimed at the ground. You had no real intention of wounding him."

"It is curious," I said, "That one often achieves one's best ends obliquely. You are right—I had no intention of leaving Paris, but fate forced my hand. Fate brought me here, and delivered me to Roche's so that Oscar Wilde might be taken by a whim and I might be taken to Copplestone's house....and brought face to face with my destiny. That is what destiny means, if it means anything at all: the improbable chain of happenstance and coincidence, which brings a man to the one and only place in all the world where he might be....shall we say *inspired*....with a vision of his true self, and his only conceivable future."

THE HUNGER AND ECSTASY OF VAMPIRES

He was staring at me now, wide-eyed. I did not have to meet his gaze; no true mesmerist requires an awesome stare or a bright and spinning object to captivate the imagination of his victim. As to whether a mesmerized man can be instructed to do something flatly contradictory to his own will....who can know what a man's will might permit, and what it might forbid? I felt that I could tell the Great Detective any lie I cared to, now, and make him believe it.

I was in a mood to be bold.

"Listen to me, my dutiful friend," I said, in a velvet-smooth tone. "Listen to me, and I will tell you the *real* truth...."

I told him, very painstakingly, that everything Arminius Vambery had said about me was true: that I *was* a vampire, and must be destroyed. I told him that his nagging doubts would linger for a while, but that he would be possessed by a perfect certainty once he had left my house.

I told him that once the certainty came upon him, he must make his plans. I instructed him to return, between one and three hours after dawn, armed with a wooden stake, which he must drive through my beating heart.

I told him not to be afraid—that he would find me unconscious and unresisting. I assured him that I would not crumble to dust, but that he would find my body lighter by a least three stones than it was at present, and that this would be an unmistakable proof of all that I had said.

I told him that he would be doing the world a great service in freeing it from an unholy evil, and that the act of my destruction would make him the hero he had always longed to be, even though no one would ever know what heroism he had shown.

THE HUNGER AND ECSTASY OF VAMPIRES

By the time I finished, he was nearly asleep. It was apparent to me that his rest cure had been terminated too early, and that he ought to have remained a little longer in that happy inactivity. I was able to take the gun from his uncannily steady hand. I checked the chambers; it was indeed fully loaded. I put it back in his hand, and gently roused him from his trance.

"Go now," I told him, gently. "Come back after dawn. You will know then what you must do."

He looked at me in bewilderment. For a few moments he did not know quite where he was or why. He put the gun away, but I had to help him with his coat and hat. When I opened the door for him, he departed meekly—but he recovered himself sufficiently as he descended the steps to turn and face me, and say: "This matter is not yet finished, Count Lugard. Depend on it."

"I do," I assured him, as I raised my hand in a salute of farewell. "I do depend on it."

I watched him from the doorway while he disappeared into the shadows of the night. There were still three hours and more until dawn.

* * * *

22

I collected my case, took a candle from the sitting-room, and went down the steps into the cellars of the house. The nearer ones to the foot of the stairway had been wine-cellars once, but I had stripped out the racks when I had installed the false doors, and had thrown them away. What need had one such as I of vulgar intoxicants?

Laura lay in her coffin, perfectly at peace. Her wan face was lustrously clear and her dark eyes seemed almost luminous. The small star-like mark on the cheek beneath her left eye stood out very clearly. Her lovely hair was neatly gathered about her finely-chiselled features.

"Soon," I whispered. "Soon, my love!"

She did not wake while I did my work; she might as well have been truly dead. She did not even wake when I pricked her arm with the needle, and slowly injected the drug into her arm.

"Never fear, my love," I said to her. "There is a better world for such as you and I, and a path which might lead us there, hand in hand. I have laid my last nightmare, played my last trick, and now the time is come for expiation and redemption. I have found my destiny, and I know at last that it is within my grasp."

I found that I was weeping, and wiped the tears from my eyes with my sleeve. How could I, or any other man, ever have thought that I was heartless? How could I, or any other man, ever have condemned me as a monster, forever doomed to remain outside the human community, a thing made shabby by mockery and misfortune?

I filled the syringe again with the remainder of the portion of Edward Copplestone's elixir of life that I had so carefully made up and measured out.

No one else would ever be able to use it, unless the world produced another man with Copplestone's peculiar fascinations—and even then, the colonial powers would have to refrain meanwhile from obliterating the ancient but precarious wisdom of the tribesmen he had visited.

I *knew* that there would be no such man, and no such reprieve for the custodians of wisdom. The future for which I was bound was indeed the future of destiny. Nothing could threaten its masters now, whether or not they had the power and the wit to take protective action on their own behalf. I had saved them. I had made the world safe for vampirekind.

I was as certain that no one else could follow us into that glorious world where violent, vapid mankind was naught but a myth and a memory as the Great Detective was that I was a vampire who could and must be destroyed by a stake through he heart.

Before taking my appointed station and injecting the drug into my own arm I reached out to touch the cold forehead of the lovely victim of my lust.

I wanted to feel the faint warmth of her forgiveness before I escorted her into the misty reaches of the worlds beyond the world.

THE HUNGER AND ECSTASY OF VAMPIRES

"We leave nothing behind but a sunless world of dismal madmen," I told her, softly, "and we are bound for the vivid and effulgent future, when we shall revel and rejoice in the hunger and ecstasy of vampires!"

* * * *

Afterword

I was once at a conference in Nice where the amiable John Dean, stricken as if by shellshock, told me that he had just had a conversation with the redoubtable Darko Suvin about the people in Shakespeare's plays. It had, apparently, been a short conversation; as soon as the subject was raised Professor Suvin had fixed poor John with a stern and steely gaze and said: "There are no *people* in Shakespeare's plays; there are only narrative *devices*."

I hope that I made sufficiently soothing noises at the time, but now it is time to come clean. Darko Suvin was right; there are no people in works of fiction—there are only narrative devices. Even when the characters in works of fiction wear names which were, in our own world, attached to real people, and even when the characters in works of fiction have biographies which echo the biographies of their real namesakes in every ascertainable particular, they remain mere narrative devices. The world of a story is self-contained and it consists entirely of text; it is not our world and it has no people in it.

This does not, of course, serve to protect writers from recriminations, as Jean Lorrain (the person, not the narrative

THE HUNGER AND ECSTASY OF VAMPIRES

device employed in the prologue of *The Hunger and Ecstasy of Vampires*) found out. He was indeed called out by Guy de Maupassant after Maupassant objected to what he considered to be a demeaning caricature of himself in one of Lorrain's books. By the time Lorrain had to meet Marcel Proust in 1897 about a little matter of a nasty book review he had been summoned to at least one other duel, although—in keeping with the etiquette of the day—any shots that were exchanged were discharged harmlessly into the ground. In the end, of course, it was the courts that laid him low; his one-time friend Jeanne Jacquemin sued him for damages after he based one of his characters on her and brought him to the brink of ruin.

Fortunately the dead are immune to libel. They have no defence against the use of their names as narrative devices, and are hence reduced to spitting in their graves. (I say "spitting" because, whatever proverbial wisdom may allege, the dead are like the lilies of the field: they toil not, neither do they spin.) Unless Sir William Crookes was right about the inevitability of his survival after death and is disposed to haunt me, none of the real people reflected in my narrative devices has any means of objection to my representations. For politeness' sake, however, it might be as well to set straight one or two small matters of record.

* * * *

Assuming that such narrative devices as Oscar Wilde's travelling plans are a faithful reflection of the similar schemes of the real individual there are sufficient indications to be found in the Count's narrative for us to determine exactly when the events it describes took place. Were the hearers of his tale as well-informed as we are, they could be quite certain that

THE HUNGER AND ECSTASY OF VAMPIRES

Professor Copplestone began to tell his story on the evening of 12 January 1895. The question of who "the hearers of his tale" might be is one to which I shall return.

In our world, as in the world of the story, Bram Stoker did meet Arminius Vambery in 1890, when Vambery visited the "Beefsteak Club" which Stoker had established to entertain friends and admirers of Henry Irving. Vambery was professor of Oriental Languages at the University of Budapest and had travelled extensively in the far east. When Stoker, prompted by a bad dream, began seriously to research the folklore of vampirism it was to Vambery that he naturally went for much of the information which he used in constructing the character of Count Dracula for the book that was eventually issued in 1897. Vambery presumably provided the model for Professor van Helsing. So far as I am aware, however, Arminius Vambery the person—unlike Arminius Vambery the narrative device—had no daughter named Laura and was not in the habit of inventing or disseminating malicious rumours.

In our world, M. P. Shiel and H. G. Wells were not personally acquainted with one another in 1895, although Shiel had met Oscar Wilde several times, dining with him on one occasion at Roche's in Soho. It is almost as unlikely that Shiel, had he received an invitation such as the one described in the story, would have whipped off a telegram to Mornington Road as it is that Wilde should have solicited the company of some obscure East European Count with a shady past and an unfortunate penchant for fighting accidentally-homicidal duels.

It is perhaps not so very unlikely that Sir William Crookes might have sought moral support from Nikola Tesla, had Tesla happened to be in London in the course of one of his several European trips—in our world, admittedly, he wasn't—but I must confess that Tesla is only in the plot because English science fiction writers must take care to introduce at least a modicum of "American interest" into their plots, lest their books should seem too remote from the parochial concerns of the hard-headed customers who control the world's biggest sf marketplace.

All of this is, of course, straightforward; what is not so straightforward is the manner in which the remaining characters in the story—the "good doctor" and his friend the grey-eyed "Great Detective"—relate to our world. They clearly have no direct analogues within it, but they do bear a suspicious resemblance to certain narrative devices used by a real writer. Narrative devices are better protected against abuse than real people; their protection under copyright law does not lapse, as the protection of libel law does, upon their deaths, and it is therefore important for me to establish that the "suspicious resemblance" in question is no mere imitation.

The "Great Detective" of *The Hunger and Ecstasy of Vampires*, whatever his name might be, is definitely and obviously *not* the titan of *The Strand* that we have all learned to love and respect (far better, I dare say, than we could love or respect any actual individual who was alive—or, as the whim of his author dictated, in limbo—in 1895). *My* narrative device is an entirely different and far less fortunate individual who has to share his own world with a narrative device which reflects him in much the same way that Guy de Maupassant and Jeanne Jacquemin were reflected in novels by Jean Lorrain. It is plain that he has suffered far more than they ever did from the unease consequent on being forced to shoulder the burden of a mythical *alter ego*, and we must not judge him too harshly.

* * * *

THE HUNGER AND ECSTASY OF VAMPIRES

It is, of course, quite unthinkable that a narrative device like Oscar Wilde would tell a *trivial* lie, so we must accept that in the world of the story Professor Copplestone really did supply Edward Tylor and James Frazer with useful information, and I dare say that both *Primitive Culture* (1871) and *The Golden Bough* (1890; later editions vastly extended) would have been better books by virtue of his input.

Contemplation of this matter naturally leads us to wonder what influence the existence of Copplestone—and for that matter Count Lugard—might have had upon other inhabitants of the world of the story, particularly those fortunate enough to hear Copplestone's remarkable story. This is, in a way, a silly question—almost as silly as asking questions about the people in Shakespeare. The world of a story has no existence whatsoever beyond the boundaries of the text; the narrative devices within it have no future beyond that which is specified therein. On the other hand, *The Hunger and Ecstasy of Vampires* does raise certain philosophical queries regarding the relationship which the future has to the past, and I hope I may be permitted a little imaginative latitude.

(If the reader's response to his mild request is that I may not, the reader might care to bear in mind that I'm the author and that this afterword is part of my text; "the reader" is therefore nothing but a narrative device within it.)

Is it possible, I wonder, that an H. G. Wells stimulated by this futuristic extravaganza might have maintained his preference for far-reaching scientific romance over stubbornly-blinkered futurology a little longer? Might M. P. Shiel have become even more eloquent on the subject of overmen even earlier in his career? Might Oscar Wilde have challenged the Marquess of Queensberry to a duel instead of a libel action, and perhaps shot him dead with a lucky ricochet? Might the good doctor have contrived to reproduce Copplestone's formula in spite of its theft by Count Lugard and donated it to humankind as a key instrument of technology? Might the vampires of the story's future—whether it turns out to be a future of destiny or one of mere contingency—find a way to reach back into their own past much as Copplestone found a way to reach forward into his future; and, if so, how would they use that ability?

The possibilities are endless—but then, they always are. That, after all, is the whole point of the sciencefictional imagination.

Which brings me back, by an admittedly roundabout route, to the question of who the addressees of the Count's tale might be. Gardner Dozois, who was one of the editors who rejected the shorter version of this narrative (which eventually appeared in *Interzone* in January/February 1995) offered as one of his reasons the unease engendered by not knowing how the Count was able to tell his story.

Given that the Count is merely a narrative device, it is not obvious that the world of the story actually *needs* an audience to whom he might be speaking, or that he *must* have survived his reckless experiment in order to be able to tell it, but I shall not quibble over such minor matters of propriety.

The Count was, of course, correct in his daring—some might say mad—endeavour. He and his substitute beloved really were projected into the far future, and they really were trapped there when the mesmerized Great Detective obligingly returned with his wooden stake and put an end to the imaginary threat of Vambery's "Count Dragul", *alias* Count Dracula. I fear that I am unable to say whether the future in question was the same one that was visited by Professor Copplestone, because there was no settlement within the text as to whether the hypothetical world of the story had its destiny built into it or whether it is as gloriously contingent as our own, which surely has not. All we can be sure of is that he arrived *somewhen*, and that there were narrative devices there, avid to hear the tale of his adventure.

* * * *

By way of closure, it might be worth recording that the title of this *nouvelle* has a curious and mildly amusing history.

When my novel *Young Blood* (1992) was in production at Simon & Schuster (UK) the editor in charge of it wrote to me saying that the sales department didn't like the title. They thought that it would be easier to shift copies if I could think of an alternative which contained the word "vampire". I wrote back suggesting that *The Hunger and Ecstasy of Vampires* might do the trick. Scrupulousness encouraged me to add, however, that if the substitution were in fact made an extra paragraph ought to be added to the Acknowledgements page, saying:

"The author would like to thank the sales staff at Simon & Schuster (UK) for pointing out that my original title for this novel, *Young Blood*, however appropriate to the text, was insufficiently sexy to hold its own in that perfervid hotbed of competition which is the modern British bookshop."

My editor at S&S decided to go with the original title after all. I don't know why. Perhaps she thought I was being sarcastic—for reasons I can't quite fathom, people often think that of me. In any case, I thought the substitute too good to waste, so I wrote another story for which it would hopefully be perfect.

* * * *

THE HUNGER AND ECSTASY OF VAMPIRES

It is nowadays considered *infra dig* to attach an explicit moral to a story. Writers' handbooks and writers' workshops alike have trumpeted forth a clarion call against the practice, and I would no more dream of posing as a non-conformist than Oscar Wilde would have dreamed of posing as a Somdomite [sic] (whatever that is; can it be possible that the Marquess [sic] of Queensberry [sic] couldn't spell?). As far as I know, though, there is no rule—formal or informal—which says that an author's afterword cannot have a moral attached to it, and the notion may even be charmingly original.

The moral of this afterword is that our images of the past, like our images of the future, are so polluted, perverted and confused by our hopes, our fears and our fancies that there is in the end no reliable method by which we might cut through the dancing veils of uncertainty to expose the dull and naked truth.

—Brian Stableford